AF292046

CASEY SUE THORNTON

WAYNE M. HOY

authorHOUSE

AuthorHouse™
1663 Liberty Drive
Bloomington, IN 47403
www.authorhouse.com
Phone: 833-262-8899

© 2020 Wayne M. Hoy. All rights reserved.

No part of this book may be reproduced, stored in a retrieval system, or transmitted by any means without the written permission of the author.

Published by AuthorHouse 07/30/2020

ISBN: 978-1-7283-6930-3 (sc)
ISBN: 978-1-7283-6928-0 (hc)
ISBN: 978-1-7283-6929-7 (e)

Library of Congress Control Number: 2020914491

Print information available on the last page.

Any people depicted in stock imagery provided by Getty Images are models, and such images are being used for illustrative purposes only. Certain stock imagery © Getty Images.

This book is printed on acid-free paper.

Because of the dynamic nature of the Internet, any web addresses or links contained in this book may have changed since publication and may no longer be valid. The views expressed in this work are solely those of the author and do not necessarily reflect the views of the publisher, and the publisher hereby disclaims any responsibility for them.

Cover Art by the author's daughter, Theresa Susanne Ysiano

CHAPTER ONE

Casey Sue Thornton woke with a start. For a moment she couldn't remember where she was or how she had gotten here. Her horse had broken its leg as she descended that rocky ledge and she had been forced to put the poor animal out of its misery. And then had started the long walk, half carrying, half dragging, her saddle. Exhausted she had stopped to rest in this little thicket of brush at the edge of a grove of trees that provided her with a sheltered covert in which to hide. Feeling as safe as this lonely expanse of high country permitted she had stretched out and had promptly fallen asleep. But something had awakened her. She lay listening and immediately there came the thud of hoof beats followed by the sound of voices, harsh and biting from just beyond her hiding place. Slowly she sat up and reached for the Winchester lying next to her.

"I reckon this is as good a place as any. Boys throw that lariat rope over thet limb and let's get this over with."

"Boss, I don't like the feel of this," came a second voice.

"Shut up Red! Didn't we catch him dead te rights?"

"I reckon you did," a third voice interjected hoarsely. "But Witimore ain't paid me in over two months, and I was flat broke. I had to have some money. And it ain't like nobody's done it; even yourself, Goodman."

"Maybe so, Kincaid, but if I did nobody's ketched me. Haw! Haw!"

Casey Sue rose to her knees and peeked between the willow leaves that surrounded her covert. Five horsemen had ridden up to a tall leafy cottonwood about twenty paces from where she hid. One of the riders had his hands tied behind his back and sat on a fine looking strawberry roan. He was young probably not much older than herself; tall she imagined, lithe of limb with wide shoulders and clean-cut jaw that at the moment was rather colorless. As she watched one of the riders tossed a noose over his head knocking his sombrero to the ground. His hair was a dark brown and lay in soft curls at the nape of his neck.

"Goodman, you're not gonna go through with it?" asked the doomed rider on the tall roan, huskily.

"Yu bet, Kincaid. Yu're a rustler," Goodman sneered. He was a big shouldered man with ruddy cheeks and an ample paunch overhanging his belt.

"You're a liar!" ejaculated Kincaid.

The rider who had tossed the lariat gave it a careless jerk tightening it about the cowboy's throat. He flinched and swallowed hard.

"What are you going to tell *her*?" he cried. "We both know that's why you're doing this. Go ahead and string me up you no-good bastard. She'll find out. Red here'll give you away!"

"Aw, Gus," imposed the rider named Red. He was as pale as the rider on the roan, and it was obvious he wanted no part of the lynching.

"I told yu te shut up!" Goodman growled nodding to the rider who held the rope. With a casual fling he threw his end over the limb above Kincaid's head then dismounted and picked it up.

Cocking her Winchester and thrusting the barrel through the willows while still remaining out of sight, Casey Sue yelled, "Drop the rope!"

"What the hell!" Goodman snarled twisting with a violent start to peer at the stand of willows.

"Drop it!" Casey Sue yelled again.

"Who the hell are yu?" Goodman demanded.

Although the rider didn't let go of the lariat he nevertheless made no move to secure it to the nearby sapling.

"Sounds like a kid, boss," the rider said.

"Show yourself, boy!" Goodman ordered.

"I'm going to tell you only one more time, Mister. Drop that rope!" Casey Sue yelled.

The rider with the rope complied, but at the same time reached for the holstered Colt at his belt. Without a hair-breath hesitation Casey Sue fired aiming at the man's shoulder. Letting out a strangled cry as his gun went flying to land in the grass, the man staggered back against the cottonwood blood spurting from the bullet hole in his shoulder.

"I told him to drop the rope," Casey Sue called out. "Now you fellers shed your guns. Toss 'em over here by me."

The hell you say—"

Goodman's reply was forcefully cut off by Casey Sue's second shot which sent his sombrero sailing off his head.

"Gol-dang!" he cried recoiling mightily one trembling hand stabbing to his head manifestly to determine if he was bleeding.

"I won't tell you again!" Casey Sue shouted.

The rider Goodman had referred to as Red was the first to comply. The other two quickly followed flinging their guns where she had directed.

"You there, Red—"

"Yea, kid?"

"Cut that feller's hands free."

"Yu got it," he replied and dismounting hurried to obey.

Drawing a jackknife from his pocket he carefully severed the cord around the rider's wrists. Once the man on the tall roan had his hands free he jerked the noose from about his neck and flung the rope angrily to the ground. He then swung from his horse and stalked over to where the men had tossed their guns and after a quick search picked up one of the Colts, apparently his own that had been taken from him earlier. He turned and peered at the place where Casey Sue still remained hidden.

"I shore thank you, kid, whoever you are," he said with obvious gratitude. "I reckon you saved my hide. I'll keep an eye on these fellers, you can show yourself now." He stood slightly sidewise hand inches from his holstered Colt. The significance of his stance was not lost on Goodman and the others.

Casey Sue hesitated a long moment. Maybe this rider was a rustler, but she knew enough to suspect that he was no worse than any number of now honest ranchers who had once burned their brand on a few mavericks. It was for that reason she had interceded. She just couldn't watch them hang this cowboy no matter what. Slowly she stepped out from behind her covert.

Brazos Kincaid looked at the youth who he guessed to be no more than fifteen. There were holes in his battered old black sombrero pulled well down shading big, deep eyes of a hue Kincaid could not discern. He had a handsome face, tanned darkly gold. Through one of the holes in his sombrero peeked a short curl of golden hair. He had shapely brown hands, rather small, but supple and strong which were now confidently clinching a Winchester still pointed at the other riders. The end of a heavy gun sheath protruded from under his buttoned up jacket. He wore overalls, high-top Mexican boots, and huge spurs all the worse for long service.

"My name's Brazos Kincaid, what's yours?" Kincaid asked shifting his gaze back to Goodman and his companions.

"You can call me Case, Case Thornton," the youth acknowledged.

"Well, I'm rite glad to meet you Case Thornton," said Kincaid.

"Wal, I reckon yu've bit off more'n yu can chew, boy," Goodman snarled sarcastically. "Shore yu must be a rustler yurself helpin' this calf stealer."

"I'm no rustler, and I just reckon I'm a better judge of men than you are," retorted Casey Sue, with even more sarcasm.

"Like hell yu are! But Kincaid hyar ain't worth fightin' fer."

"I reckon you fellers had better ride off," Kincaid interjected. "Jackson there needs to see a doctor."

"We're goin' an' yu can go te hell, both of yu—"

"Gus, I reckon your just sore 'cause I queered you with Betsy Gale," Kincaid sneered, then suddenly called out, "Hold on Goodman!"

The rider jerked his horse to a halt.

"What air yu up to?" he demanded.

"Gus, I reckon you took something off me, and I want it back," Kincaid said dryly. "There was sixty-five smackeroos in that billfold you snatched from me. Fork it over."

Goodman's face reddened in angry amazement. He stared a moment more, then reached in his vest pocket and pulled out a worn leather billfold which he tossed to the ground at Kincaid's feet.

"Much obliged," Kincaid said quickly checking the contents. He gave a satisfactory nod and watched as Goodman wheeled his horse and spurred him into a trot then breaking into a lope. The others followed.

Once they were out of sight, Kincaid whirled to face Casey Sue.

"My God, boy!" he burst out in overriding relief. "Goodman would have hung me—but for you!"

Casey Sue took a step back at the cowboy's heartfelt outburst.

"I couldn't just watch them hang you," she replied almost shyly.

Kincaid looked around. "Where'd you come from, boy?"

"Back there," she said with a jerk of her head. "I lost my horse this morning—broke his leg coming down a rocky slope a ways back. I had to shoot him. I footed it here and hid in those willows to rest. And then you fellers came along."

"By God, I'm shore in your debt. I owe you my life, Case. Where you headed?"

"Yonder," she said nodding west.

Kincaid looked quizzically at her. "You traveling alone?"

"Yes."

"No family?"

She shook her head.

"Well, I'll be. All alone, huh. You an orphan, boy?"

"I suppose you could say that."

"Well, I shore ain't about to hang around this here neck of the woods. I reckon I'll tag along with you—"

"I reckon not. I travel alone," she replied lips firm.

"See here, Case, I reckon you ain't got a choice. I owe you my life. You can't get rid of me—not until I've made it up to you. We're pards now."

"Don't be ridiculous," she exclaimed. "You don't owe me anything! And I don't want a partner. I've a matter that I've got to take care of, and I don't need company."

"Well, now," he drawled, pulling out makings and beginning to roll a cigarette. "You're a strange kid. Smoke?" he asked offering her the finished product.

She shook her head. He shrugged and putting the smoke in his mouth struck a match with his thumb and lit it, puffing out a neat blue ring.

"Sounds like serious stuff—this business you're bent on doing."

"It is. I reckon you'd just get in the way."

"I beg to differ," he shrugged easily. "Even though you're just a kid—you must be all of fifteen years old, ain't you?"

"Shore," she replied, with a little laugh, "I'm all of fifteen."

"—granted you can handle a gun," he said nodding to the Winchester she held. "But I'm a grown man and not a slouch with a Colt, and I shore would have been a goner without your help. So I reckon whatever you're up to, I can lend a hand."

"I don't want your help," she said emphatically, jaw set determinedly.

"No matter, I ain't leaving you out here alone. You just told me you had to put down your horse. What're you planning to do, walk all the way to Big Springs? That's the closest town and it's near twenty miles."

"What about your girl?"

"What girl?"

"The one your stole from what's-his-face."

"Betsy Gale? Ah, well, I reckon it'll break her heart, but it can't be helped," he grinned sanctimoniously.

She just stared at him as if he was rather tiresome.

"You got a sweetheart, Case?" he asked ignoring her as he ground the cigarette butt under his boot heel.

"No."

"A handsome feller like you? What's the matter, ain't you woke up to girls yet? When I was your age—er, never mind," he finished with a sly wink.

She took a deep breath and exhaled. "Shore that big roan can pack the two of us, but not my saddle and pack too," she said.

"No problem," he smiled. "I'll just make a travois."

"All right Mr. Kincaid, just to the next town. After that we'll be even."

'Like hell we will,' he thought, but all he said was, "Call me Brazos."

Casey Sue watched Brazos out of the corner of her eye as he went about hacking down two saplings to use as a travois. She decided his appearance belied the boyishness that seemed to be born of his careless, free insouciance. He was tall, close to six feet she guessed. His age must be near twenty-five years. He was not so lean and rangy as most horsemen, with wide shoulders and muscular round limbs. He struck her as a remarkably able horseman. All his leather trappings were ragged and shiny from use, particularly the gun holster which hung low on his right hip. The ivory handle of his Colt was yellow with age while the gun itself shone, as did his Winchester, with the bright luster of worn, polished steel. She would have to watch herself around this man, she told herself.

CHAPTER TWO

t didn't take the two of them long to construct the travois which consisted of a platform made of sturdy boughs and two saplings for shafts, leaving the ends dragging on the ground. Kincaid shot the youth an occasional glance as they worked on the travois recalling the furtive, if not hunted look in the boy's big, dark, deep eyes when he had asked him about his family. What sad and tragic experience had forced this boy to face alone the hard and bloody range? And just what was this secretive undertaking that he didn't want or trust Kincaid's help with? He felt a sudden affinity with this sad-eyed kid, and it wasn't wholly the fact that the boy had saved his life.

The big roan was a little skittish at first when the contraption was tied to his saddle, but soon settled down. Securing Case's saddle and canvas pack along with his own bedroll and pack on the small platform, Kincaid stepped into the saddle and kicking his left foot free of the stirrup reached a hand down to the boy. After a moment's hesitation the youth put his foot in the stirrup and swung easily up behind him. The little calloused palm, the supple fingers that closed like steel on Kincaid's shot a warm and stirring current up his arm and he quickly released his grip feeling momentarily unsettled and not sure why.

By the time they had finished the travois it had been late afternoon and twilight found them still several miles from the settlement of Big Springs. They made camp for the night in a thick stand of willows near a small stream.

"You think what's-his-name will trail us," Casey Sue asked quietly from her place back from the camp fire. She sat leaning against a tree, legs outstretched.

"You mean Goodman?" Kincaid replied. "Is that why you picked this out of the way patch of willows to make camp?"

She shrugged, her only response.

"How long you been on your own kid?"

She didn't answer right away, contemplating how much to tell this man. She decided to lie. It wouldn't do for him to know how recently she had started on this trail, all by herself. A lie would be the easiest way.

"A while."

His keen eyes studied her from over the flickering flames of the camp fire. She ducked her head tucking in her chin hoping he wouldn't see her furtive act for what it was. She knew nothing of this man other than what her gut feeling told her, although he talked Texas, that, at least, was something. But she had survived this far by being cautious, not trusting anyone. She had no idea what this cowboy might do if he found out she was a girl and not the boy he obviously thought. She was thankful she had recently worked on a ranch and before that wrangling horses on a cattle drive north where she learned to handle horses and guns.

She swallowed. The Lord only knew how much she had staked everything on this scheme—her future—her life.

"What's the matter?"

"Huh?" she started glancing up at him from under the brim of her old sombrero.

"You shore looked like you was doing some deep thinking," Kincaid said.

"Oh, I reckon I was. I don't know much about you, Mr. Kincaid," she replied.

"I could say the same for you, kid."

"Yes, that's true," she agreed voice soft.

"Except you saving my life like you did says a lot." He leaned back on his elbows. "Well, then, would you want to hear something about me?" he drawled.

"That's up to you," she said.

He was silent a moment longer.

"Well, I reckon you're not the only orphan hereabouts. I was reared over near Bendera. When I was fourteen I rode my first trail drive with McKeever. When I got back I discovered Comanches had raided our place. Both my folks were dead. So from then on I was on my own. Spent some time in Mexico. That was good and bad for me. I reckon I was reckless with my trigger finger. Dog-gone it there was always some hombre that needed shooting. This here last job I had though, I was almost happy. There was this girl, Betsy Gale—I reckon you heard me mention her. Well, dang it, Case, I reckon I kind of liked her. 'Course I've always had a weakness for girls, and I reckon they just can't keep their hands off me either," he chuckled, a bit smug she thought. "But Witimore, the feller I rode for, never paid us for near two months. I ain't no rustler, Case. I branded a few mavericks, and I reckon you know that's not crooked. But I admit it's my conscience that accuses me, 'cause I knew in my heart none of them calves were mine."

He paused to toss a branch on the fire, which flashed up brightly, and by its light Kincaid had a better view of the boy's face. The hard and bitter expression appeared softening.

"But hell, kid, I had to have some money—"

"Shore, I reckon you needed to spoon Betsy Gale," she broke in.

"Dang if you shore ain't a wise cracker, kid," he said with a solemn shake of his head.

Casey Sue got to her feet and absently brushed off the back of her pants. "I reckon I'm going to turn in. It's been a long day," she said.

Kincaid watched as she moved a ways back among the trees where she unrolled her bedroll. She sat and pulled off her boots and unbuckled the bulky gun belt and laid it next to her and then stretched out on the blankets.

"You're not a rustler—at heart," she said soberly, and turned on her side facing away from him.

Kincaid admitted he was somewhat puzzled and nonplus over this strange orphaned lad who seemed so out of place on this wild range. He had kind of figured that by sharing something about himself, the boy might do the same. It just wasn't something a feller did—asking another man about his past. If he wanted to divulge it he would. Case Thornton, it seemed, was keeping mum. Well, so what. The boy had saved his life. A man just didn't disregard something like that. The kid was stuck with him now. He'd figure a way to repay him if it took the rest of his days. And whatever this quest was the boy was bent on— Brazos' interest was piqued.

He recalled his first glimpse of the youth when he stepped out of the bushes. In his excitement the boy had faced them straight-on whereupon Kincaid had a clear view of the lad. He was surprisingly young. Although his tanned cheeks had a slight vestige of downy beard he looked like a pretty girl, notwithstanding the strong chin, the almost stern lips. His eyes were large and very blue, almost purple. Kincaid lay back on his blankets. The boy knew how to handle a gun, and wasn't afraid to use it that was for certain, but it still remained…he was just a kid. He just might need his assistance whether he wanted it or not. With a weary sigh he rolled into his blankets.

Kincaid was brought abruptly awake by the sharp crack of a rifle. A moment later there was a second shot. The sun was just topping the low hills sending pale red shafts through the willow leaves. He sat up darting a swift glance around. The space where the boy had spread his blankets the night before was empty. Heart thumping Kincaid rolled out of his blankets and had just slipped on his boots when the youth stepped into the clearing. He held two rabbits in one hand, his Winchester cradled under the other arm. His old black sombrero was pulled down low on his forehead.

"I'll have breakfast ready in a jiffy," he called without appearing to look up.

Kincaid was suddenly aware of the delicious aroma of boiling coffee. A smoke-blackened tin coffee pot sat between two rocks over a blazing fire. Dang he must have slept like a log. That realization scared Kincaid. He prided himself on being a light sleeper. How long had the boy been up anyhow?

"I reckon I slept in," he muttered.

"You shore did," she said somberly. She dropped the rabbits on the grass and leaned her rifle against a tree.

"Here, Case, I'll skin those," Kincaid said.

"It's no trouble. I'll do it," Case replied sinking to her knees and pulling a jackknife from the pocket of her jacket. Soon the dressed-out rabbits were sizzling on the end of two sticks propped over the fire.

"You're kind of a handy feller to have around," Kincaid said around a mouth-full of flavorsome rabbit meat a short time later. It seemed only a moment before Kincaid looked up to see the boy was wiping his hands on his pants.

"Dog-gone, Case, you shore must have been starved," Kincaid declared.

"I was hungry," Case admitted and set about cleaning up.

A short time later they were underway, and for most of the morning Kincaid entertained his traveling companion with tales of his amorous conquests, which for the most part elicited only a few brusque comments from the other. Fortunately for Casey Sue he couldn't see her redden cheeks and disgusted grimaces. It was nearing evening when they rode into Big Springs dragging the travois. Rising out of a slight depression to higher ground the grey stone buildings and wood shacks of the town came into view. Half hidden by green trees the bluff of the Pecos could be seen beyond. As Kincaid drew nearer he made out a number of houses that he did not remember from the last time he visited the place.

"If I remember right there's a hotel not far down the street. I reckon we could get rooms there for the night," Kincaid said glancing back over his shoulder at Casey Sue.

For a moment she made no response. She had never traveled this far south and supposed she wouldn't meet anyone here who knew her. Nevertheless, she certainly didn't want to risk being recognized, not as the girl she was. That would only bring trouble. There were difficulties, however, that stood in the way of her desires. She needed to buy a horse and she had almost run out of food supplies…and she was hungry. Moreover she was coming more and more to realize she wasn't up to doing this on her own. There was so much she didn't know…too many unknowns; things that she could hardly imagine that had kept her awake on many nights. And in addition, she didn't know much about her new-found "pard". It was risky being in his company. His grey eyes were too sharp. Still, it would be so easy to trust him. He was so damn persistent—just because she had saved his life.

"I reckon I could go for that," Casey Sue finally replied.

"There's a stables on the far end of town. Say, it ain't none of my business, but do you got the dough to buy yourself a horse?"

"Yes. Is there a general store?" She'd see about buying supplies later.

"Yep," he said and pointed with his chin toward a tall boarded store front they were just passing before which a heavy wagon and several sleepy horses stood. A sign in large faded letters read: *General Store, Geo. Rockfort, Proprietor.*

"I reckon we ought to get something to eat first off," he added. She had no argument with that. "There's a place at the end of the street. A little Mexican café. Juan Torres and his two daughters run the place. I'll set you up with Margarita. She's the youngest, but I reckon she's as hot as one of them red Mexican chilies. I bet you two will hit it off grand."

"I'm not interested in your little *señorita*," she said dryly.

"Not interested! What's wrong with you boy?" he demanded incredulously.

"It's cause of my dear ma'ma—"

"Your ma'ma?"

"Yep. I promised her I'd, you know, save myself for marriage. Aw, I reckon she'd turn over in her grave if I broke that oath," she sighed plaintively.

"So you say," Kincaid said struck by a significance in the moment for which he was unable to account for.

The little café was not crowded and they took a table in one corner. A Mexican girl perhaps sixteen approached the table. Her black eyes flashed with recognition as they settled on Kincaid.

"*Señor* Brazos," she exclaimed happily. "Carmen missed you. Why you stay away so long?" she pouted sensuously.

Casey Sue caught herself just in time before rolling her eyes.

"Howdy, Carmen," Kincaid said. "So you missed me, huh?"

"*Si, Señor* Brazos. Why you no write a letter like you say?"

"Why, I reckon I figured I'd beat the letter," he grinned. "Here I am. Carmen, meet my new pard, Case Thornton. Case this here is Carmen. Her papa owns the place."

"*Señor* Case," she smiled warmly arching a dark eyebrow, long dark lashes fluttering.

Casey Sue gave a stilted nod. "Hello, Carmen," she acknowledged feeling Kincaid's eyes on her.

"Well, Carmen, we shore are hungry enough to eat one of them beefs you got out back," Kincaid said. "How about a big thick steak and three eggs? Make it the same for my pard."

Several customers entered the café and much to Casey Sue's relief Carmen was too busy to rejoin them. Hunger satisfied they left the café and sought the hotel on the next street. It was a two story structure and appeared surprisingly well attended. Casey Sue was prepared to argue anticipating that Kincaid would suggest a single room. Thankfully he did not but instead rented adjoining rooms on the second floor. After depositing their packs in their respective rooms, Kincaid rode to the stables at the far end of town to see to his horse.

While he was so occupied Casey Sue ordered up a tub of hot water. She hadn't had a bath in days and was actually salivating at the opportunity. It took the two young Mexican girls several trips to fill the tub with steaming water. Once the tub was filled and the room at last empty, Casey Sue sat before the cloudy mirror and dipping her fingers in a small jar of grease removed the downy fuzz of stage makeup off her chin and upper lip. She was glad she thought of this part of her disguise. The hint of whiskers was, she realized, an added bonus. She hesitated. Perhaps she should have left it on? She shook her head. She wanted to sleep undisturbed tonight. The makeup itched. Besides it wasn't like she was sleeping in the open. She was well protected in a hotel room, and that bed looked so inviting.

With the fake fuzz removed, she stripped tossing her dusty pants and shirt over the chair, and settled with a glorious sigh into the tub letting the heated water lap luxuriously about her chin.

After soaking for some minutes just enjoying the experience denied so long, she reached for the bar of soap and began scrubbing humming to herself. She uttered a gasp as the door suddenly swung open and

Brazos Kincaid stepped into the room. She cursed under her breath. She had forgotten to lock the damn door.

"Hey, get out cowboy! Can't you see I'm taking a bath!" she shouted. Her heart thumped madly as she sunk down in the water until only her head showed above the foamy water lapping up over her chin, and at the same time wrapping her arms across her chest. Thank God, she breathed, realizing the soapy water effectively hid her.

"Did you hear!" she demanded her face a bright red and such a blaze of purple fire flashed upon Kincaid that he took a step back.

"What's the hell's wrong with you, kid?" he exclaimed staring at the boy.

Absent the old black sombrero the lamplight shown on her big eyes and flushed face and especially the rebellious golden curls. What a singularly handsome lad! He looked younger than the fifteen years he had confessed to. His thin cheeks glowed rosily. It struck Kincaid that his lips were too red and curved for a boy, but his eyes—cornflower blue, were his most marked feature—keen but at the moment flashing purple.

"There ain't nothing wrong with me," she declared sarcastically. "I just like my privacy. So if you don't mind…"

"Hell you say," he replied passing from surprise to tease. "On the shy side, huh?" He grinned. "Okay, I didn't know you was so modest, Case. I'll go and leave you to enjoy your bath. I'll see you in the morning."

Casey Sue waited a full ten minutes before resuming her bath fearful that Kincaid might decide to return. Scrubbing her hair and rinsing off the soapy water, she finished her bath and stepped out of the tub wrapping a large fluffy towel about her. All the while she kept a wary eye on the door. It had no lock, a worrisome fact she now perceived recalling Brazos Kincaid's uninvited entrance. That, she tried to assure herself had been a fluke. He wouldn't try that again…would he? Donning a long cotton nightgown she sat before the mirror and stared at her face. Had he saw through her disguise? How strangely he had stared at her.

A soft knock on the door startled her, but then she relaxed as she heard the soft feminine voice speaking in Spanish. She crossed to the door and opened it to admit the two Mexican girls who had come to remove the wash tub. She waited until they had completed the task and had departed then shaking her short damp curls resignedly; she blew out the lamp and slid under the blanket with a satisfied sigh. She stretched wiggling her toes. It was glorious to feel like a girl again. She suddenly sat up as Brazos Kincaid's handsome face flashed before her eyes. She glanced quickly at the door. There was no way to lock it. She let out an annoyed sigh and slid her legs over the side of the bed. She scooted the only chair in the room over to the door and braced its sturdy back under the door knob.

"I reckon I'll feel a little safer now," she breathed and before crawling back in bed she felt the pocket of her coat for the envelope wrapped in oilskin. She patted it protectively.

She lay staring up at the ceiling, tired but now wide awake remembering her Uncle Will, the way he looked when she had found him. She shuddered, tears stinging her eyes. He had been stabbed—in the back, his pockets turned inside out. She didn't believe for one minute that he had been set upon by robbers that the town marshal asserted. She knew better. They were after what was in her coat pocket. She would stake her life on it. She knew she was taking a risk traveling alone. Would they guess she had the document…and the map? Well, if they did they would be looking for a young woman, not a scruffy kid…she hoped.

Oh, what plans her uncle had. They had sat up most of the night while he talked his eyes bright with excitement. In a few months they would be so rich they could travel the world, live in the best hotels if she liked…or buy that ranch her paw had always wanted…ah, he had been so full of life. But now she had plans of her own. She'd find her uncle's partner, this claim they shared together. She had sworn on her Uncle's dead body; she'd find him and get what was coming to her uncle. There were two of them, the murderers. She was sure of that, but she had only got a good look at the one as she passed him on the stair. She would never forget that face. They hadn't found the claim form and the map. She was sure that was what they sought. The thing was, they could well be after her now. She'd have to be careful. And she still wasn't sure if she could trust Mr. Brazos Kincaid.

First things first, though. She couldn't go anywhere without a horse. She'd have to purchase a good sturdy mount, like that big roan of Brazos'… And out of her slowly draining cache of greenbacks… then, somehow dissuade Brazos Kincaid of the silly notion that he was indebted to her. What she had to do, she'd do alone. She had never really had friends—except for Mr. Brasee. And as far as family, there had only been her paw and Uncle Will since she was fifteen. So it wasn't such a big deal. She brushed away the tear gliding down her cheek with the tip of her fingers.

CHAPTER THREE

When Casey Sue woke the window across from her bed revealed the gray light of dawn. After a moment she slid out of bed and walked to the window on bare feet. From the vantage point of her second floor room she could see over the trees the muddy mist-cloaked Pecos River. It frowned forbiddingly, notwithstanding its sinuous breadth. West beyond the river lay a wild untamed country that proudly boasted its lawlessness, and beyond that laid the equally wild territory of New Mexico. She wondered absently if there was a ferry across the river or if she would have to ford it. From this distance it didn't look all that formidable. She had gone over and over in her mind this whole mess and it seemed to her that her uncle's murderers must have known about his strike and followed him from New Mexico. So, not finding the document they sought they most probably would now be on the lookout for her. But why didn't they accost her there on the stairs? They must have noticed her. Maybe they didn't recognize her…hadn't known her relationship to her uncle. Well, it probably wouldn't take them long to figure that out. And when they did they would most likely reason that she would set out for New Mexico to acquire her share of her uncle's gold claim. But then, out of the blue, a smidgen of doubt entered her mind. It troubled her. If her uncle's murderers had indeed followed him from New Mexico, why had they waited so long before attempting to steal the gold claim papers?

She turned from the window and after washing, dressed in her boy's togs then sat before the cloudy mirror and opened the makeup kit and began to painstakingly apply the wispy beard and mustache. The sun was just peeking over the horizon when Casey Sue picked up her Winchester and slung her pack over her shoulder. She quietly opened the door of her room and surveyed the empty hall. Tip-toeing down the hall to the stairs she mentally cursed the jingling spurs that she had neglected to remove. She didn't want to wake up Brazos Kincaid, her self-avowed pard, and have him insisting on tagging along with her.

She spied the little café where she had eaten last evening with Brazos and decided she had best eat before undertaking her venture into the wild country west of the Pecos. She glanced in that direction as she stepped up on the boardwalk before the café and a sudden sensation, as though someone had walked over her grave, caused her to shiver. It was gone as quickly as it came and she pushed open the café door. A shrill laugh greeted her ears and a young Mexican girl flounced past her dark eyes sparkling with mischief as she shot a glance back over her shoulder at a table occupied by three cowboys in dusty range garb. They were young and handsome as cowboys go despite faces ruddy from wind and sun, and obviously full of deviltry.

Casey Sue took a seat at a vacant table on the opposite side of the room and a moment later the same Mexican girl approached. She was pretty. Casey didn't recall seeing her the evening before.

"Buenos dias, Señor," she beamed. "What will Margarita get for you?"

"I'll have ham and eggs, two I reckon, over easy, and a cup of coffee," she said.

The girl nodded giving her a bright smile and pranced off casting a playful glance at the three cowboys as she went. So that was Margarita. Brazos had hinted he wanted to fix her up with the little *señorita* last evening. That would not have gone well, she thought with a disgusted shudder. When her meal came Casey ate quickly. Finished, she paid her bill and slinging her pack over her shoulder and with her Winchester in one hand started off for the livery stables.

The day was going to be warm she realized reaching the cool interior of the barn where she dropped her pack and glanced around.

"Howdy son," came a voice from behind her and she turned to see the tall rangy figure in a colorful shirt, worn overalls and boots.

"Howdy," Casey Sue replied.

"Gonna be a scorcher," the man said, wiping his forehead with a multicolored neck scarf. He glanced at her pack. "I reckon by the look of yu, yur not fixin' to hang around our little town."

"No, sir," she said.

"Whar's that tall puncher yu rode in with yesterday?"

"I reckon he's still sleeping."

"Hmm. Yu figurin' on headin' out by yourself?"

"Yes, sir. An' I'm shore in need of a good horse."

The man pulled makings out of his vest pocket and began rolling a cigarette. "Smoke?" he asked offering her the tobacco pouch.

"No, sir. I don't reckon I've took up the habit."

"Good fer yu, son. It shore is a bad practice," he said eyes taking in the Winchester she held in one hand and the holstered barrel of the pistol protruded from under her buttoned up jacket. "So, yu're lookin' fer a good hoss?"

"Yes, sir."

"Whar yu from, son?"

"Nowhere, I reckon."

"Hmm. Lone cowboy, eh? Thet's interestin'. Whar're yu headed?"

"West," she said.

"West, huh? Thet's some rough country fer a young feller all on yur own."

"Yes, sir. That's what I been told, but I shore got business there."

The man gave her a long intense look. It took all her willpower not to shift uneasily under that hard scrutiny.

"I reckon there's all kinds of shady hombres hidin' out in them breaks," he said after a moment. "Yu wouldn't be thinkin' of turnin' te the bad would yu, son?"

"No, sir, I shore ain't. I swear on my—mama's grave," she said solemnly.

"Wal, I reckon I believe yu, son. Let's walk on out te the corral out back."

Casey Sue followed him outside. She was becoming more confident in her male disguise but still held her breath when people stared at her too intensely. She stepped up to the fence and peered into the corral. It held only one horse.

"Wal, what do yu think, son?"

Casey Sue was quick to observe the horse was not a mustang, but a larger and finer breed than the tough little Spanish variety. It was a magnificent animal, black as coal, clean-limbed and heavy-chested, with the head of a racer.

"Gosh," she exclaimed before she could catch herself, "He's shore superb!"

"My name's Chad Hopkins," he remarked leaning both forearms on the top rail. "Yu got a handle, son?"

Casey Sue darted him a look. "Case Thornton," she said.

"Pleased te meet yu, Case Thornton."

"Likewise, Mr. Hopkins."

"Wal, now. I got thet hoss last week from a feller owned a spread north of here by the name of Gage Sinclair. I reckon Sinclair's sellin' out an' ain't had time te take care of 'em lately. Accordin' te Sinclair thet hoss had the run of the range. There ain't been a leg thrown over 'em fer a year."

"What's his name?" Casey Sue asked.

"Don't reckon he's got a name far as I know. I reckon whoever buys 'em will have te name 'em."

"What are you asking?"

"Two hundred."

"Whew," Casey Sue whistled. "I reckon he's shore worth it, Mr. Hopkins, but I shore can't afford him," she said wistfully.

"Wal, I didn't figure yu could," he replied his gaze sliding over her battered old black sombrero and baggy jacket. "An' I don't reckon thar's nobody hyar 'bouts thet has thet kind of money 'ceptin' a feller by the name of Wheeler. He shore wants thet hoss bad, an' I reckon he's just biddin' his time waitin' fer me te give in an' sell 'em at his price, which is shore a steal on his part an' he's damn shore laughin' behind my back 'cause he knows it." He turned his head and gave her another piercing look. "Make me an offer, son."

Casey Sue sucked in a deep breath. "Mr. Hopkins, I reckon all I could come up with is…fifty bucks." She said the last with a hopeless sigh.

"I'll take it."

She looked at him, speechless.

"Did I mention I don't much like Wheeler?"

The voice was cold, full of disdain. "Where the hell did I find you two idiots?"

"Ah, we was in the cantina—"

"Shut up, I'm talking!"

"But yu said—"

"Quiet!"

"It weren't our fault. The old man never had them papers on him like yu said he would," the man growled scratching at the stubby bristles covering his nearly razor-sharp chin. The man was tall, almost skeletally thin with shrunken cheeks and eyes that protruded freakishly from their small sockets.

"Alright, I heard you. The girl must have it. Find her and get that document! You think you can handle that?"

"Shore, we know what te do, don't we Buck," he grumbled darting a glance at the man beside him. He was balky of shoulders, ruddy of face, and his dark thin hair fell over his brow, almost to his large ghoulish eyes. For the rest he had a long, sharp nose, a small mouth from which a bold scar extended to the tip of his peaked chin.

"I reckon we're gonna need a stake, we're flat busted," that worthy said spitting a stream of brown juice into a corner of the dingy room.

"Alright, but you better not fail me, understand?"

"Shore, we understand." the man returned with a toothy grin.

Bright sunlight poured through the lone window across from his bed when Brazos Kincaid woke. He sat up rubbing his eyes with the heel of his hands. He was still somewhat flummoxed over this queer kid who called himself Case Thornton. The boy was obviously shy, but it was difficult for Brazos to accept that he would be opposed to girls. Maybe part of the answer lay in the reason why the boy was on his own in this rough West Texas country. And it probably had something to do with him not being brought up in this corner of Texas. There was a hint of East Texas in the boy's speech, maybe even Louisiana. Still, even so, there was just something peculiar about the boy that Brazos couldn't quite come to grips with. He stretched, yawned. He hadn't meant to sleep so late, but he had been worn-out. He smiled recalling Carmen's lush charms.

"That gal can shore kiss," he grinned.

Humming a tune he slid out of bed and washed and dressed. Buckling on his gun belt with its row of shiny brass cartridges and plopping on his sombrero, he stepped out in the hall and crossed to Case's room and knocked on the door. There was no answer. He tried the door and it opened. He peered inside.

"Reckon he's down gettin' breakfast," he muttered darting another look about the room. He didn't see the boy's pack. "You don't reckon he's—"

Returning to his room he snatched up his own bedroll and pack and hurried down the stairs. He wouldn't put it past the boy to set out on his own on whatever this undertaking was he was on. And he had more than hinted he didn't want or need Brazos' help.

"Well, Case Thornton, pard, we'll see about that. You'll not get rid of me that easy," he said aloud as he took the steps two at a time.

The boy was on foot. So first off he'd have to buy a horse and the logical place to start looking would be the livery stables.

Not far out of Big Springs an unfrequented trail branched off the road north. No wheel had ever rolled along that trail, or a herd of cattle ever tramped its dusty cactus-bordered course, Casey Sue decided. She stayed on the more traveled road which led down to the banks of the muddy river. She reached and smoothed the horse's silky mane. According to Mr. Hopkins the big black hadn't been ridden in well over a year and so she had been a little leery the horse might hang her on a fence. But the big black took Casey Sue's mount easily, pranced and champed a little, and tossed his head. It had seemed to her that something akin to affection had passed between horse and rider as would two old friends. It had been love at first sight.

Once out on the road she discovered that the big black, who she decided to name, *Satan*, was a fast walker and had an easy trot. It struck her that no horse in the country could approach him in speed and endurance.

"Gosh, I should ride back an' give Mr. Hopkins a big kiss!" she exclaimed grinning jubilantly.

Of course that would have shocked the old man to the toes of his scruffy boots, and for sure blown her disguise. She was still halfway of a mind to do it no matter. But then she might run into Brazos Kincaid and eventually have to explain her business. He would probably try to talk her out of it, and that she wouldn't have. She wouldn't allow anything or anyone to stop her.

There was no ferry across the river. The Pecos appeared shallow though, however, swift moving. Without more ado Casey Sue headed Satan into the river taking a slight diagonal course downstream toward the opposite shore. Satan was a big and powerful horse; moreover he had enjoyed a rest of several weeks. And he apparently liked water. He crossed without swimming. They splashed up on the opposite bank with only the bottom of her boots wet.

She rode up into a stand of willows out of sight of the trail. From there she surveyed her surroundings. From all she'd heard, this country west of the Pecos was rampant with outlaws and other unsavory characters. She didn't want to be surprised by any such hombres.

Near the river thick groves of willows abound, but as she moved away bearing always west it became bare grass alternating with scaly patches of greasewood and cactus and a few scrub oak. Later in the day the country before her became ridged and began to show cottonwoods here and there in the hollows and yucca and mesquite on the higher ground. Here among the cottonwoods she halted and drank from her canteen. The thought suddenly occurred to her that perhaps she should have gone north before turning west and in that way avoiding this wild desolate country and the constant fear she would run into outlaws or desperadoes. But this had been the shortest, straightest course and she had already lost enough time.

The sun was setting and twilight descending on the cottonwood grove. Slow running water splashed softly over stones in an adjacent streambed. Rounding a slight curve in the path Casey Sue smelled smoke the same instant she saw the fire. She quickly drew rein, but too late. Three pairs of eyes jerked in her direction. Two men squatted on their hunches before the fire, a third stood opposite them. The two before the fire got quickly to their feet, hands hovering over their holstered Colts. There was nothing now for her to do but bluff her way as she regarded the three with coolness she didn't feel.

"Bust me if thet ain't Sinclair's hoss," one of the men by the fire exclaimed.

The man who had been standing took several steps toward Casey Sue. He had a forbidding face which showed yellow eyes, an enormous nose, and skin the color of dust, with a thatch of sandy hair. He seemed to squint as he stared at her.

"Hey kid, who are yu an' where the hell did yu get thet hoss?" he demanded. His yellow eyes took in the big black gelding then finally turned their glinting, hard light upward to her.

"If it's any of yore business, I bought him," Casey Sue retorted.

"It shore the hell is muy business!" he snarled eyeing her menacingly. "Ain't nobody in the whole county got money te buy thet hoss, an' fer shore not a snot-nosed kid like yu."

"Well, mister, I reckon you're wrong," she replied curtly. "I bought him from Mr. Hopkins at the livery stables just this mornin'."

"Oh, yeah? How much?"

"Fifty bucks—"

"Fifty bucks! Har. Har," he guffawed tossing a look over his shoulder at his two comrades, which elicited corresponding chortles. "Wal, boy, muy name's Buck Wheeler, an' I been after old man Hopkins te sell me thet hoss fer near two weeks, an' he wouldn't part with 'em—not fer less than two hundred. I reckon yu stole thet hoss, boy!"

"I bought this horse. I reckon you'll just have to take my word for it," she said sharply, though her heart thundered in her chest. Her grip tightened on her Winchester and with her thumb she eased back the hammer. There were three of them. And the thought occurred to her—how would this big black horse react to gunfire?

"Wal, I ain't takin' yur word fer it, savvy, boy?"

Once up on the opposite bank of the river, the tracks of Case Thornton's horse were easy to follow. Brazos knew he wasn't too far behind him. It had paid to talk to Chad Hopkins. He now had a trail to follow. He had lost some time buying a few supplies but by the looks of these tracks it wouldn't be long before he overtook Thornton.

The boy was shore determined venturing off through this wild country all on his own and him just a youngster, Brazos considered as he rode along. Not many men, let alone a green boy hazarded west of the Pecos—unless they were desperadoes or outlaws or them bent on going to the bad. Was that what was driving Case? Was he running from the law? Had he already gone to the bad?

The boy just didn't strike Brazos as one of those thrill-seeking youth wanting to make his mark on the world. Yet, he had to admit, he was somewhat puzzled and nonplused over this soft spoken Texas youth. Was it his eyes? Brazos had been struck by the sad haunted look he saw in those large blue eyes so dark they were almost violet, and yet those same eyes could blaze with purple fire as he recalled the boy's fury when Brazos had surprised him in his bath. Brazos chuckled remembering how Case's face had flushed a brilliant red. Gosh, if looks could kill! Shore, Case had lived alone most of his life, Brazos mused; that accounted, he reckoned, for what seemed the boy's unusual, even peculiar agitation.

Brazos' reverie was interrupted by the sound of voices, angry voices. He drew rein listening and soon surmised the situation. He edged his big roan forward until he could see around the curve in the path. Case sat on a big black horse his Winchester across his lap. Not twenty paces away crouched a heavy-shouldered man, hand suspended above his holstered Colt. Behind him just beyond the small fire were two others. He gently prodded his horse and the animal rode into the clearing.

The big man's attention was suddenly diverted to Brazos and he saw the hesitation in his yellow eyes. Brazos dismounted and threw his bridle.

"Case, pard, what's the trouble here?" he asked coolly.

"Who're yu?" demanded Wheeler.

"Name's Brazos Kincaid," he replied curtly. "An' that's my pard, Case Thornton."

"Yeah, an' is thet suppose te mean sumthin te me?"

"I reckon it ought, 'cause I'm shore getting fed up with your bluster," he drawled taking a sideways step that was either lost on Wheeler or disregarded. "What you want with my pard?"

"Wal, since yu've made it yur business—thet big black hoss he's ridin'. I reckon he stole it!"

"Wheeler, you're a liar!" Case spat.

Brazos saw it in an instant. This yellow-eyed Wheeler intended to kill Case. There was no sudden animosity driving Wheeler. It was just his chance to get the horse he wanted and he intended to kill to achieve it. But he now had to face Brazos and the situation had suddenly changed. He no longer faced a fresh-faced youth whom he thought to easily intimidate. He knew Brazos was neither, but he had weighed his chances and figured the odds were in his favor.

Brazos felt like iron and yet thrill after thrill ran through him. It was a situation long familiar to him. He was aware of Case Thornton out of the corner of his eye. The boy knew how to use that Winchester he carried, but had he ever killed a man? Brazos had sincere doubts. Wheeler's two companions worried him. He'd have to pick his shots quickly and accurately. And Case could be an asset or a liability. The last in that Brazos' concern for the boy's safety could slow his own reactions.

"Case, pard, why don't you ride out of here," he said coolly.

"Ump-umm," Case rejoined.

"Thet's right, Mister, he ain't goin' nowheres," Wheeler growled.

Wheeler remained motionless; his eyes pale and steady, his right hand like a claw. That instant gave Brazos a power to read in his enemy's eyes the thought that preceded action. When Wheelers hand moved Brazos' gun was spouting fire. Two shots both from Brazos' gun—and Wheeler fell, his gun exploding as it hit the ground and dropped loose from stretching fingers. At the same moment Brazos felt a blow—a shock—a burning agony tearing through his breast. A second bullet whistled close to his head as he snapped off two more quick shots and saw beyond the fire the man go down. Even as he flung his hand up for another shot he realized the third of Wheeler's companions had ducked out of sight into the brush surrounding the cottonwood grove. A moment later came the thud of horse hoofs moving away at a run, then all was still.

"Damn you, Brazos, you could've let me get a shot off!" Casey Sue ejaculated shock and dismay coloring her words. Then her voice faltered. "Brazos—your shirt's all bloody!" she cried leaping from the big black.

With Case's words Brazos became aware of two things; the hand he instinctively placed to his breast still held his gun, and he knew he had sustained a terrible wound. The clean-cut hole made by the bullet bled freely both at its entrance and where it had exited. He coughed up a reddish-tinged foam. He stumbled to his horse catching up the dragging reins.

"Mount up," he ordered and swung into his saddle. "Let's ride! I reckon that hombre's gone for help."

As they rode, Casey Sue felt like her heart was going to burst from her chest. She was still trying to gather her wits; still in breathless awe by Brazos' blinding speed and deadly precision. She had realized Wheeler's intent—it was plain in his yellow eyes. He was going to kill her—for her horse! And fury had momentarily blinded her to all else. Her focus had been on shooting Wheeler, but it had all happened so fast, and two men were dead—and she had not even fired her Winchester. With pale face and mute lips she stared at him.

"Your wound—we have to stop!" she said.

He nodded. "Wanted to get away—they'll—be after us." He turned his dark gaze on her. "Case, pard, I reckon I'm—bad shot."

CHAPTER FOUR

They rode on and before long Brazos could not see the trail or hear his horse. He did not know if they traveled a mile or many times that far. But he was conscious when the horses stopped, and had a vague sense of falling and feeling Case's arms before all became black to him. Consciousness returned and slowly he opened his eyes. He sensed he was in some kind of hut made of mesquite branches. It had a stale musty odor and he decided the place was old, constructed some time ago, months, maybe years. He saw their saddles and his pack and one he recognized as Case's against the near wall of the hut beside a pallet of blankets—Case's bed. He had no idea where he was and a strange ethereal feeling, like waking from a bad dream he couldn't quite remember, weighed upon him. He felt weak and had no desire to move and presently his eyes closed and he slept.

He was awakened by a noise like metal clinking on rock and saw Case kneeling off to the side a tin plate in his hand.

"Brazos," she cried setting the plate aside and scooting over next to him.

"Howdy, pard," he rasped. "How are you, and how am I?"

"I'm fine—no thanks to you, Brazos Kincaid! An' it's about time you come to," she replied gruffly as though the boy found it difficult to talk, Brazos thought.

"I'm going to live then?"

"Your wounds are mostly healed, Brazos, but you've been awful sick."

"I have, huh."

"Yeah, fever."

"Fever? How long have we been here?" he asked meeting the boy's gaze. He was struck by the look of strain and dark hollowness of his eyes.

Casey Sue reached past him, picked up his sombrero and dumped some pebbles out on the blanket. She made a point of counting them. "Seven days," she answered.

"Seven days!" he exclaimed, disbelievingly. "I been sick all that time? An' you nursed me?"

"Yes. And I thought you were going to die I don't know how many times. Damn you, Brazos Kincaid for scaring the daylights out of me!"

"Aw, you look upset, worried you'd lose your pard?" He gave her a lopsided grin. "Well, Case, I don't seem to remember much after that little gun fight. Tell me, how'd we get here?"

"I stumbled on this place just about dark on that first day. There weren't nobody chasing us yet, so I figured it best to stop. You fell out of your saddle and I dragged you in here an' stopped your bleeding. I—thought you'd die that night. But in the morning you was still living, an' that gave me some hope. When your wounds closed over an' you started breathing easier I figured you'd get well quick. But then you got feverish. You shore raved; called out a whole slew of names—mostly female, and—a bunch of other stuff. It's a good thing there weren't nobody chasing us or your wild talk would have shore led them here. I think it scared me most though when you was quiet. I didn't know if that breath would be your last. An' every day I put a pebble in your sombrero."

"Whew-ee," he exclaimed! "You did all that?"

She shrugged.

"Say, where's our horses?"

"I hid 'em in a grassy park a little ways off down the slope. There's water nearby."

"So, we weren't followed?"

"Might have, but I reckon the rain shore helped, washed out our tracks."

"It rained?"

"Yep, off an' on for three days."

"Lucky the roof's sturdy—"

"Humph! It leaked like a sieve."

"But everything looks dry," he puzzled glancing around.

"That's 'cause I stretched both our slickers over the roof. Water dripped in a little around the edge though, but not much."

"Well, I'll be a son of a gun! Case Thornton, you stuck with me, saved my life—again. I reckon now we're shore pards for life," he said gravely.

She stood and left the hut without speaking. She walked down the brushy slope a short ways before sitting down and drawing her legs up to her chest and wrapping her arms about them. As she had rode behind him that first day she had considered how best to deal with Mister Brazos Kincaid, and at the time had decided that it would be best to keep him rigidly at a distance. She had been determined to go on alone. But it looked like she was stuck with Brazos Kincaid. The knucklehead had decided they were pards for life having once again saved his life. No doubt she had. Who else would have forced water down his parched throat, bathed him when he was burning with fever and insensible. At the time, though, she had been too frightened that he would die, than to worry over his nakedness. She took a deep breath feeling her cheeks flaming, remembering. But how could she have not stayed with him? She couldn't very well abandon him; let him die.

It had been exceedingly fortunate that she had stumbled upon this old hut. Obviously it had been constructed by a fugitive—one who meant to keep an eye both ways so as not to be surprised. There were two openings, one at the front and the other at the back. And it was close to water. A clear spring was only a few yards down the slope. Thank goodness for that, and plenty of grass for the horses. Yes, she had probably saved Brazos Kincaid's life, but then he had saved hers as well. Wheeler would have killed her, she had no doubt. She'd bring up that fact, but he would just argue that one cancelled out the other. It still remained that she had saved him from being hanged.

She uttered a curse under her breath. A bird sang overhead. Blue sky shone brilliantly above the scrub oaks. She had lost a whole week's time. She rested her chin on her drawn-up knees. But it seems fate had been toying with her all along. Damn Brazos Kincaid! He was so damn handsome, and the way he looked at her. Ah, he probably made all women feel like that. He did it without even trying. It brought out that hidden yearning in her—the kind that wished he would take her in his arms and…What was she thinking, he didn't even know she was a woman! He thought she was a boy for Heaven's sake! Life was complicated enough as it was. How was she going to deal with that? She couldn't hide her sex from him forever especially if they continued traveling together, spending nights on the trail. She forced herself to think, forced her heart to beat at a steady pace.

For just a moment she wanted to go back inside and take his hand and confess everything. But she couldn't bring herself to move. She suddenly realized that if she left him now it would leave a hole in her heart. But what did that signify next to her oath? She mustn't let him have any impact on her. She was untouchable. She was hard and unswerving, like a rock. She had to be. Rock was unyielding. She had her job to do.

She got to her feet and went back inside the hut.

"You hungry?" she asked.

"I should smile," he said, pushing himself gingerly up onto one elbow.

"There's still some rabbit stew left—"

"You went rabbit hunting?"

"Well, I was leery of using a rifle in case some of Wheeler's bunch was still on our trail, so I set out snares. Game's shore plentiful here 'bouts. There's deer come of an evening for water," she said busying herself arranging a smoke-blacken pot over the small fire. "I'll heat up some beans, and there's canned peaches—"

"Gosh, kid, you're shore a wonder," he marveled.

She mumbled something under her breath quickly averting her gaze as she stepped outside the entrance of the hut where a small fire smoldered. Brazos braced himself on one hand watching the boy. He wasn't wearing the old black floppy-brim sombrero, Brazos noted and sunlight glistened with crimson brilliance off the mass of rebellious golden curls atop his head. He frowned as he eyed the lad recalling certain things that had seemed peculiar about him, like how unreasonably upset he had become when Brazos had innocently barged into the hotel room to find him taking a bath. Scowling, still at a loss as to what it was that troubled him, Brazos threw back the blanket intending to rise only to let out a yelp.

"Hey, pard, what the hell happened to my clothes?" he demanded.

Casey shot a look back over her shoulder. "I washed 'em. They was covered in blood," she returned. "An' I reckon you were burning with fever. I—had to cool you down—somehow or other," she acknowledged, unassumingly she hoped, as she ducked her head so he wouldn't notice her suddenly flushed cheeks.

"Well, I reckon that explains it," he grunted giving her an odd look. "Where's my clothes anyhow?"

"Yonder by your saddle," she said not looking up. And she kept her eyes averted acutely aware of the rustle of blankets as he carefully stood.

She waited marking the sounds as he dressed. His movements were slow; his breathing labored making it all too obvious he had not yet regained his full strength. Shortly he came and in typical cowboy fashion hunkered down beside her. She wished she had put her old sombrero back on wary of the way he gazed at her, but she had grown relaxed without it while he was feverish and unaware. She heaped a serving of stew on the tin plate and handed it to him not looking up, and then served herself. They ate in silence.

"Damn, that was shore tasty, Case. Where'd you learn to cook so good, anyhow?" Brazos said laying the plate aside.

"You were starved that's all," she replied.

"I shore won't argue with that," he grinned, "But that don't account for your cooking."

"I reckon it were my Uncle Will," she said stacking their plates off to the side.

"Uncle Will, huh? He shore must've been a good cook."

"He was terrible," she chortled. "All he knew how to fix was sourdough biscuits and beans. I got so tired of eating beans; I figured I had best take over the cooking 'fore I went batty."

Brazos chuckled. "So, you lived with your Uncle Will, huh. What happened to your folks?"

She was silent for a moment her deep dark eyes taking on a furtive almost haunted look. She shook her head. Her story was a long and sad one, but she realized she would have to tell him at least some part of it. She'd just have to fudge a little on the dates.

"My mother died when I was twelve—swamp fever paw said. You see we lived on a plantation near La Grande Pointe along Bayou Teche—that's in Louisiana. Things never were the same after the war and when mama died paw decided to come west. So, my Uncle Will, paw and me, we left Louisiana. We had a canvas covered wagon, and eight horses. I rode and drove for months I reckon. Somewhere near San Antonio Uncle Will left us. Paw said we was going too slow to suit him. He said Uncle Will would meet us at the next town." She broke off her face taking on a grim cast. "He never showed up, and then Paw—he was bit by a rattlesnake over near Sweetwater. There wasn't no doctor. He—he died two days later."

"Damn, Case, you was just a twelve year old kid—" Brazos cursed softly.

"I reckon by then I was thirteen," she said darting him a look. Actually, at the time, she had just turned seventeen, but she wouldn't tell him that bit.

"What'd you do?"

"Well, I sold the wagons and all but one of the horses," she continued with an angry lift of her chin. That's when she had decided she'd be safer dressed like a boy. "I got a job wrangling horses for a trail-driving outfit headed up to Kansas City. When that drive was over I come on back to San Antonio with the boss, a fella by the name of Abe Brasee. He were from Louisiana too, so we kind of hit it off. I was shore happy there. Last spring Uncle Will showed up at the ranch. He didn't know about paw's death. He'd felt he had let me and paw down, but he swore things would be much better. He had a place o'er New Mexico. We'd have a home of our own—" She broke off suddenly, stared off into the distance.

"Hmm," he murmured. Stretching out his long legs he leaned back on one elbow. "So, your uncle finally caught up with you, after what, two years…"

She nodded.

"What happened? Why'd you wind up on this lonesome trail?"

She didn't look up. "Things didn't turn out like he planned. Two weeks later—" she swallowed looking up and then as quickly looking down again.

Brazos was struck once again by the lad's handsome face, tanned darkly gold and big eyes that suddenly appeared furtive, if not haunted.

"Uncle Will was murdered—"

"Ah, kid. Murdered?!"

"You bet it was murder," she snapped, eyes now flashing blue fire. She abruptly scrambled to her feet and stomped off down the hillside looking all at once proud and stalwart in her dark buttoned up coat golden curls flashing in the sunlight.

Brazos watched her stalk off. What a sad story! The poor kid, left all on his own!

"Well, pard," he muttered grimly. "I reckon it's settled, I ain't about to let you go off on whatever fool errand you're on alone."

He got carefully to his feet and walked slowly down the hillside.

"Case, Pard, we got to talk," he said coming up behind her.

She tossed a sharp look back over her shoulder. "I figured I've been doing a lot of talking already," she said.

"Yea, but I reckon we need to talk about this here trail you're on—"

"You ain't talking me out of it!" she snapped turning to face him her chin taking on a stubborn line.

"Hell's bells, kid! Simmer down. I reckon I'm coming with you. It's got something to do with your uncle's murder don't it."

Deep inside a feeling of relief welled. She wouldn't be alone. But almost as sudden as that feeling sprang up it wilted. He was only coming along because he felt indebted to her. His heart really wasn't in it.

"You don't have to do this, Brazos. I reckon we're even up," she said meeting his eye.

"Un-huh, Case. We're pards, boy, don't you know. Where you go, I go," he drawled easily, but there was a hard look in his eyes that boded no argument. "Now, why don't you fill me in?"

So, she told of returning to the hotel rooms where she and her Uncle Will were staying and passing two men on the stair. One had caught her attention by the very strangeness of his appearance. He was almost pencil thin, and his protruding eyes seemed huge above sunken cheeks. The other man she could not describe, her gaze had been drawn solely to his companion. She had quickly moved past them and hurried to her uncle's room where she found him sprawled on the floor…dead, his pockets turned inside out and the room a mess. Contents of drawers had been tossed on the floor, the bed's mattress drug aside.

"What were they looking for?" Brazos queried a keen look in his gray eyes.

She shouldn't have mentioned the ransacked room. The words had slipped out before she'd thought. Could she fully trust this man? Even with all they had gone through? She was suddenly assailed with doubt. She had been betrayed and abandoned so many times… She shook her head dropping her gaze.

"Hmm, so you figure them two hombres you passed on the stairs were the ones that murdered your uncle?"

"Yep, I'm shore of it. I'll never forget that face, them eyes," she said, emphatically.

"Dog-gone, Case, you weren't going after them murderers all on your own were you?"

She nodded. Let him think that was her purpose. She wasn't about to tell him about the gold claim…not yet anyhow. Her uncle was a dreamer. Maybe there wasn't anything to it anyways.

"Well, it's a damn good thing we crossed paths," he returned grimly.

"I reckon," she smiled brushing aside the pang of guilt in the pit of her stomach.

The following morning they packed everything and set out. At the base of the hill Casey Sue halted and gazed back at the little hut where she had spent those stressful days waiting for Brazos to either die or heal. Strange as it might seem, but somehow she was going to miss the place.

The summer day was hot and drowsy. They pushed on west far into the night before halting to camp. On the afternoon of the third day they had halted by a stream. The day had been, like those before, scorching hot and Case's face seemed extra flushed.

"Case, pard, why don't you shed that coat and ride in your shirt sleeves?" Brazos queried.

"Hey, cowboy I don't have a heavy shirt like you," she retorted, "I don't want to get all sunburned and scratched up by brush."

Brazos shook his head exasperated but dismounted and proceeded to lead the horses to water after which he stripped their saddles and staked them out to graze. Coming back to camp carrying the saddles he spied Case seated beneath a cottonwood. He had removed his sombrero and perspiration beaded his flushed forehead.

"That water shore looks inviting. Come on, Case let's take a dip and cool off," Brazos shouted as he unbuckled his gun belt. He tossed it over his saddle and began to strip.

"Not me," she declared and Brazos thought his face had lost some of its color.

By the time he had his shirt off Case had disappeared under the trees. Brazos gave a frustrated sigh. He had forgotten how sensitive the boy was. Removing the rest of his clothes he dived in the water. When Brazos emerged and dressed sometime later Case was not in sight and did not show his face for a full hour.

They sat around the small fire having eaten. Brazos leaned back on one elbow stretched out his long legs and crossed them at the ankles.

"Say Case, something bothering me," he drawled eyeing her on the opposite side of the fire.

She cast him a look, but said nothing, her heartbeat quickened.

"Where are we headed, anyhow?" he asked.

"What do you mean?"

"Well, is there something you're not telling me about them hombres that murdered your uncle? You know what they were after when they ransacked your hotel room," he added.

She stared at him.

"Let me get this straight…the way I figure it you know where we're headed…don't you? And I don't reckon you're bent on catching your uncle's killers. Something else is driving you."

"Yes," she said quietly. "Well, sort of."

"Sort of, you know where we're headed…or sort of, you're not chasing your uncle's killers, or both?"

"Brazos, I reckon you'll just have to trust me," she sighed.

"I do trust you, kid. You saved my life twice now…ain't it about time you started trusting me?"

🐎

——————CHAPTER FIVE——————

Early in the afternoon from a ridge top they sighted Linrock, a green path in the mass of gray. For the barrens of Texas it was indeed a fair sight. Dusk had fallen when Brazos Kincaid and Case Thornton rode into the little town of Linrock. No one appeared to notice or mind their arrival. The town lay in a shallow valley overlooked by a distant range of mountains. Brazos entered the town with mingled feelings of curiosity, eagerness, and expectation. The street they started down was not a main one. There were small, red houses among oaks and cottonwoods. They rode clear through to the other side, probably more than half a mile. They crossed a number of intersecting streets, where they saw children playing and several women, and more than one dusty-booted man.

Half-way back from this street they turned at right angles and rode up several blocks. Saloons and gambling halls lined several wide streets. As they rode along the garrulous sound of voices interspersed with loud guffawing laughter, the clink of dice and the whirr of roulette wheels virtually drowned out the incessant jangle of piano music. They continued on till they came to a tree-bordered plaza. On the far side opened a broad street which for all its horses and people had a sleepy look. On the corner was a two story board-front hotel. On the opposite corner was a little Mexican café. It was filled with eaters but they were able to find a table in the far corner. Shortly a slim Mexican girl approached. Her lustrous raven black hair was pulled back from her forehead with a colorful ribbon, and her eyes of velvet blackness peered openly at Brazos.

"What would you like, Señors?" she inquired musically her luminous brown eyes flitting from Brazos to Case.

"Well, we're two hungry hombres," Brazos drawled. "I reckon I'll have your steak and some coffee."

"Si, Señor," she purred deep-brown eyes shifting to Case.

"I reckon I'll have the same," Case said.

The girl flashed large dusky-hued eyes surrounded by long dark lashes at Case before flouncing off with a swish of her colorful skirts.

"Say, Case boy, that little Señorita shore has eyes for you," Brazos drawled raising an eyebrow suggestively.

This brought a bright tint to the boy's cheeks Brazos noted. "I reckon she's more your type," she replied gruffly.

"Aw, don't be so shy. Go on, ask the little Señorita her name when she comes back," Brazos said nudging Case with an elbow. "She shore looks a fiery little thing."

"Shore, I reckon you're right, but I'm for a bath and off to bed. I'm shore beat," Case rejoined yawning.

"Dog-gone, I shore don't understand you, boy."

The girl returned shortly with their food.

"Say little Señorita, what's your name?" Brazos drawled, flashing even white teeth.

"Carmelita," she said prancing away with a saucy wink back over a slender shoulder.

"Whew-ee," Brazos exhaled noisily, "I think I'm in love."

"Here, you loco skirt-chasing hombre, eat up, cause I'm heading for that hotel once I've fed my stomach," Case snorted.

The hotel appeared fairly new and clean. Brazos, apparently recalling the incident where he had barged in upon the boy in the bathtub, accepted that Case was self-conscious about dressing or undressing in his presence. And so there was no hesitation about getting separate rooms adjacent to one another on the second floor. Casey Sue was glad. It had been nearly a week since they had left the little mesquite hut where she had attended Brazos' wounds and she was eager to bathe and finally be able to sleep in a soft bed once more. Besides it was becoming an extremely challenging undertaking to keep concealed the fact that she was a girl. At the café she had wanted to punch Brazos, hard. It seemed he was determined to fix her up with a girl, the pigheaded man. Well, she would just have to stay shy of cafés in the future—especially Mexican ones with pretty señoritas.

The hotel was equipped with a separate bathing room on the top floor, so Casey Sue lost no time enjoying that amenity after they had eaten supper. The warm bath acted like a mild soporific and she lay there with the steaming water lapping about her chin. Was Brazos with that black-eyed little Mexican hussy from the café? The sudden unbidden thought promptly put an end to her pleasant mood and she quickly finished her bath. Once in her room she undressed and climbed into bed refusing to waste one more second thinking about Brazos Kincaid. But the last drowsy memory before sleep claimed her was that of Brazos' intelligent gray eyes.

Brazos' strength was returning, but he was still not fully himself. The bath was particularly refreshing and he stretched out on the bed in his room allowing his thoughts to wander settling finally upon the boy in the next room. There were things about Case Thornton that he still found peculiar, that still flummoxed him. Brazos kept hoping the lad would overcome what seemed unusual agitations. He was modest almost to the extreme, yet he was determined to hunt down his uncle's killers. Brazos had to admit though that of late Case had grown less aloof, evidently glad to be with Brazos. That had caused Brazos to grow more and more attached to him. There were limits, however, recalling how the boy refused to go for a swim with him. He was obviously shy, but it was still difficult for Brazos to accept that he would be opposed to girls. Strange, it was like bringing up a boy who stayed boyish. Nevertheless these peculiarities rather endeared Case all the more to

Brazos. It was, he decided, because of a sense of protectiveness, almost guardianship that the lad inspired.

The door slowly swung inward with a soft creak and the pale shaft of moonlight through the lone window beside her bed fell upon a dark figure framed in the doorway. Casey Sue held her breath as the figure paused apparently listening for the sound of her undisturbed breathing. He took a step toward the bed. 'Damn you Brazos,' she mentally cursed. He had finally discovered her; had waited and now thought he could slip into her bed; like he could add her as another one of his conquests. Well, he had another think coming.

"Brazos Kincaid, get the hell out of my room!" she hissed outraged.

With a mumbled curse the dark figure was suddenly upon her. Something struck the side of her head—hard, sending stars flashing before her eyes. The blow sent her tumbling off the bed feet tangled in the blanket. Stunned she fumbled to sit up. Her gun was hanging over the back of the chair just arm reach away. But she never had a chance to grab it. She saw the fist coming but couldn't avoid the blow that crashed against her chin. In the instant before darkness swept over her she saw in the moon's light the sinister bearded face and piercing eyes; then she knew no more.

Brazos Kincaid lay awake staring at the shadows on the ceiling above his bed. Maybe part of the answer lay in the reason why the boy was on his own in this rough West Texas country—hunting down his uncle's killers.

A sound from the next room broke in upon his musings. Brazos cocked his head listening. It had sounded like a muted cry followed by the thud of what could have been a body falling to the floor. He sat upright swinging his legs off the bed. The noise had come from the room Case was in. Brazos pulled on his pants and crossed to the door barefoot. Other sounds from the next door room reached his ears—a heavy step moving about. Too heavy to be Case's! Slipping his Colt from its holster he opened the door and entering the corridor stepped to the door of Case's room where he put his ear against the wood panel. The sound of a gruff male's voice deep and coarse reached him.

"What the hell!" he muttered under his breath, and without a moment's hesitation thrust the door open and saw in the dim glow of moonlight from the lone window a large shadowy figure crouched over something on the floor.

"Hey there!" Brazos snarled.

But the figure with surprising quickness straightened and flung the heavy object he was holding at Kincaid's head. Kincaid managed to duck but the object struck him on the shoulder knocking him backward. Before he could right himself the dark figure bolted out the door and down the corridor his booted feet thudding on the boards. Brazos started to go after him, but checked himself. An instant later the man had disappeared down the stairs. With one last frustrated look in the direction of the stairs, Brazos stepped back into the room. His eyes now accustomed to the dim light, quickly made out the slight figure in white lying in a crumbled heap on the floor beside the bed.

Fumbling in his pocket for a match he lit it with his thumb. Glancing around Brazos spotted the lamp. Quickly raising the glass shade he lit the wick and turned to peer down at the white-clad form on the floor.

"Case, boy, you're not dead!" he cried and at the same time reached and turned the boy over on his back. With an inarticulate cry he stared down at where the thin gown gapped open exposing a rounded swelling female breast. His eyes sped downward to where the nightgown was rucked up about shapely white thighs.

"My God!" he gasped. "A woman!"

With that exclamation Brazos awoke from his stupefaction and quickly pulled the nightgown closed refastening the loosened button thereby concealing her nakedness. Then, unbidden, his mind started rehearsing everything he had said to her the last three weeks; all those stories about his love life—And he had even tried to get her lined up with the girl in the café last night, and—Margarita, one of Juan Torres' daughters! —And worse! She had undressed him, bathed his feverish body while he lay unconscious!

"Lord Almighty!" he cursed under his breath. "Making me think you was a boy!"

At that instant her eyes flickered open and he was scarcely prepared for the dark humid mystery of reviving mind and soul. But then the cornflower blue depths turned dark with terror. She struck out with tiny fists, but he caught her wrists.

"It's me Brazos," he cried.

"Brazos?" she whispered faintly. "God, my head hurts!" She sat up dizzily. "I—" She cast a slow glance about the room taking in the contents of her pack scattered across the floor and her jacket lying in a heap in one corner. That man had obviously been after *it* she realized. On hands and knees she crawled to where her jacket lay and dug into one of the pockets. She clenched the envelope wrapped in oilskin against her chest as she let out a relieved sigh. Brazos must have scared him off before he had time to find it.

"He didn't take it," she whispered.

"Didn't take what?" Brazos demanded, kneeling beside her. He gently lifted her chin, tilted it to the light. "There's a big purple bruise on your jaw. That skunk hit you!" he hissed.

She raised trembling fingers and touched her cheek, then the side of her head behind her ear and winced. "This one hurts the worse," she grimaced.

"Let me take a look,' he said, and gently eased aside a few soft golden curls. "Whew-ee! I reckon! There's a whopping knot above your ear. What'd he hit you with?" His voice was cold and filled with menace, and one could imagine that it would not have augured well for the culprit had he been within reach.

"It felt like a rock, but I reckon it was only his fist," she acknowledged with a shudder, but then her hands went instinctively to her breasts where her fingers clinched the material as though just now realizing she was in only her threadbare nightgown.

All the while he had struggled to keep his eyes from wandering to the front of her nightgown and the small peaked mounds barely concealed beneath the thin cotton. He grabbed a blanket off the bed and wrapped it about her shoulders. She met his gaze for an instant and offered him a tired but grateful smile as she tucked the blanket firmly about her. But then his gaze hardened.

"That was outrageous of you!" he hissed, as his face grew red. "Making out you was a boy! And let me tell them—them—God-awful stories—"

"Let you!" she flashed, face flaming worse than his. "You big galoot! How could I stop you?"

"Yeah, well—dang it, Case—say, is that your real name?"

"Casey Sue," she said shyly after a moment's hesitation. "Case for short."

"Ah-huh, well, shore I can see it now…that I know you're a girl," he said gallantly. "I reckon I can, you know," he shrugged. "If I can stand it I reckon you can too," he finished unobtrusively. "How long have you been masquerading as a boy anyways?"

She looked up at him and Brazos found himself gazing into dark, troubled cornflower blue eyes.

"Since I was seventeen, after paw died—"

"Seventeen?! You don't look more'n fifteen. How old are you anyhow?"

"Nineteen—and don't look at me like that! I had to earn a living and being a girl made it hard—"

"Dog-gone!" he exclaimed shaking his head.

"It wasn't always so bad—being thought a boy. Course I had to get use to hearing lots of cuss words and—and bawdy stories," she said glancing disgustedly at him.

"Aw," he groaned, head drooping, but then straightening. "Say, that story you told about your uncle finding you, and then being murdered—that's all on the square, huh!"

"You bet it is! And I'm shore glad not to be riding under false colors anymore," she sighed sincerely allowing him to lift her to her feet and guide her to the bed where she gingerly settled on the mattress. He couldn't seem to take his eyes off her delicate little toes peeking from beneath the hem of her nightgown.

"Yeah," he replied and reached and drew the chair up, and turning it around backward, he straddled it, arms folded over the backrest. "Now, Miss Casey Sue—Case Thornton, what was that hombre after?"

She darted a look up at him and for a moment her eyes searched his. She knew now, without a doubt, she could trust him. She slowly held out the oilskin covered envelope. He opened the packet and unfolding the document.

"Well, I'll be. I reckon this here is a record of a gold claim, and—this looks like a map. And I reckon your name's on the claim."

She nodded. "Uncle Will told me about the gold mine and showed me the claim form and the map to where the mine is the night he came to the ranch. He told me that he and a man named Joshua Gaines had discovered a rich vein. Once they were settled and the claim filed, Uncle Will came back looking for me and paw. He gave that to me," she said pointing to the claim form. "He wanted me to hold on to it, he said, for safekeeping. I'm shore now that he suspected he was being followed."

"Hmm," Brazos grunted. "So, are you really after them that murdered your uncle, or is it this gold strike you're after?"

She gave him a sheepish shrug.

"Ah-huh," he grunted.

"When he came to the ranch he had a woman with him; Flo Morgan. He never explained much about her—I think he was kind of fond of her, though she was much younger than him. Flo laughed a lot. I liked her. She was shore sweet and treated me nice. Well, we packed and started west the very next day. I had kind of stopped wearing boy's togs by then," she said wistfully. "We hadn't been on the trail more'n two weeks when—when Uncle Will was murdered—oh, it hurts to bring it back. Flo stayed with me 'til Uncle Will was buried then she up and left; said she was going back to San Antonio." She gave Brazos a rebellious look. "That's when I went back to wearing a boy's disguise. I wasn't about to turn back. Uncle Will believed—staked his dreams on that mine. And I swore I—I'd go find it."

"Well, I've got to hand it to you; you're shore a game kid, being a girl and all," Brazos mused softly, marveling that fate had brought them together. "Going on all by yourself like you did."

She gave Brazos a rebellious look. "This don't change a thing!" she snapped. "I'm still going! Only now I know they're on to me—"

In the lamplight her face, as white as if it had never worn any golden tan, except for the dark bruise, seemed chiseled out of marble, cold, pure, singularly noble, and as sad as her life must have been, yet determination blazed there too in eyes large, dark, luminous. But her features alone could not have accounted for the disturbing transformation from boy to girl. That white nightgown! It was thin—old fashioned, scarcely concealing the graceful contour of womanly breasts.

For a moment he could not convince himself of the facts. His wandering rides, his ruthless hand with a gun, his hapless life of meaningless drifting—these had landed him here at the side of this girl as lovely as an angel—and as good—a girl whom he owed his life.

"Damn it, Case—can I still call you that?" he asked but continued without waiting for her answer. "What have I got to do to convince you we're partners? You ain't going on without me," he avowed.

One pale shapely arm slipped from the folds of the blanket and the small hand closed about Brazos' large calloused one. It was affirmation enough for Brazos.

CHAPTER SIX

Casey Sue lay awake, as she had been for some time, watching the sleeping form stretched out in front of the door as the pale light of dawn lightened the window, remembering. Brazos Kincaid had booked no argument when he informed her that he would sleep on the floor in her room the rest of the night. Though she at first protested, she was actually glad she wouldn't be alone. The thought of that man returning, of facing him again, turned her heart cold. She hadn't slept much and neither had Brazos both being too worked-up to sleep. She had watched him blow out the lamp and stretch out on the blankets before the door. A long while later she had heard his steady breathing and knew he slept. She had dozed fitfully off and on until the gray of dawn began to lighten the window. Her head still hurt, but the piercing pain of earlier had lessened to a dull throbbing—unless, of course, she made a quick move. Brazos stirred and sat up which brought an end to her musings.

"How are you feeling this morning?" he asked eyes searching her face.

"Still a little shaken," she admitted. But she wouldn't turn back. Yet as she stared at Brazos she couldn't imagine once entertaining the idea of braving this whole thing by herself—the very thought of being alone once more, lonely and solitary, sent such a feeling of dismay washing over her that her breath caught painfully in her chest.

"I reckon I'll wait out in the hall so you can get dressed," Brazos said as he buckled on his gun belt and plopped his sombrero on his head.

She said nothing, until he stepped into the hall and was about to close the door.

"You won't go far away?" she demanded.

"Don't worry," he drawled with an easiness he didn't feel, and closed the door softly behind him. He leaned his back against the door and took a deep breath. She was a vision sitting there in bed blanket pulled up to her chin—a vision to confound not just his senses but his wits as well with her sleep-tossed golden curls and cornflower blue eyes that regarded him steadily over the top of her drawn-up knees. He had tried to read them, but the distance had defeated him. He was no stranger to women, but those eyes, even the one swollen half closed—

"Whew-ee," he muttered. "I've never seen the like. What have I got myself into anyhow?"

He went into his room, but kept the door open while he washed and shaved, his ears tuned to any activity in the hall. Finishing his toilette he glanced about the room before stepping out into the hall. Figuring he had given her enough time to dress, he tapped lightly on her door.

"It's me, Brazos," he called.

The door opened immediately and she stood framed in the opening rebellious golden curls surrounding cheeks, one of which was puffy and distended, supporting an ugly black and green contusion. She was dressed in her worn overalls and high-topped Mexican boots, her jacket buttoned up to her throat. Placing the wide sombrero gently on her head she reverted once again to her masculine disguise, absent the stage whiskers.

She stared at him openly, one cornflower blue eye black and swollen nearly closed. This morning while she washed and dressed she had done some thinking. She was grateful for his companionship; nevertheless, she would have to keep their dealings on a purely practical level. It was the only way, to suppress each and every little leap her unruly nerves might make, giving him no reason whatever to imagine he had any inherent effect on her. She knew better than to do otherwise. She was a woman and had a woman's innate intuition. Brazos Kincaid thought himself a lady's man; she didn't intend to be one of his conquests.

Brazos couldn't take his eyes off her; at the ruby lips slightly parted, at her lovely cornflower blue eyes and sweet face that the dark bruise or any amount of severe male attire could ever disguise. He abruptly hauled his mind off that track he had started down. She had saved his life and his interest in her was purely driven by the dept he owed her.

Wasn't it?

He suddenly wondered how truthful he was being.

"Say, you ready for some breakfast?" he asked smiling easily.

"Yeah, but I don't have a taste for Mexican this morning," she replied.

"Shore," he drawled not missing the sarcasm. "We'll eat in the hotel dining room."

She nodded and stepped past him.

He couldn't put his finger on what, but something had changed since he'd left her moments ago. It was as though she had erected some vague yet steely barrier. As if she dismissed him as inconsequential. He had never considered himself vain, but on the other hand, women just seemed to fall for him, so it was, for him, something new, this coolness.

"I don't reckon that hombre will try anything in the daylight," he said keeping her to his left, she noticed, so his gun hand would be free as he came up beside her. "But I reckon I'll keep a sharp eye out."

"So will I," she remarked simply, Winchester cradled under one arm.

He glanced at her and grinned. He had no doubt of that. They descended the stairs and entered the noisy dining room. Once settled at a table facing the door and their order made, Brazos leaned back in his chair surveying the room. Case's attacker could well be in this room, watching them, waiting for his chance.

"Say, Case, did you get a look at that hombre?"

"It was dark and it happened so fast. But I do remember that he was big, and I think he had a beard of some sort."

"Yeah, I recollect you saying one of the hombres you saw on the stairs the day your uncle was murdered was skinny. So this wasn't him."

"No. But Brazos I never really paid attention to stickman's companion. I'm thinking this could have been him."

"Ah-huh," he nodded lips set in a grim line.

Casey Sue glanced around the room eyeing the other customers. As best she could that was, what with one eye swollen closed. Could *he* be here? No, none of the other breakfasters fit even the vague description of the man who broke into her room. He had been big she remembered and she sensed more than saw that he had a thick beard, although nothing more distinctive. They had been after the claim form, certainly, but probably more to the point…the map. Still, how had they known about the gold strike? Had they followed her uncle? That hardly made sense. Why wait until Uncle Will reached San Antonio if they had followed him? It was the same question that continued to plague her. They would have been well advised to hold him up long before that. She shook her head frustrated, and then groaned at the sharp pain that knifed through her skull cutting short her reverie.

"You all right?" Brazos asked concerned.

"Yeah, just a headache."

"I reckon that's shore understandable," he grunted. "You feel like travelling?" The pained look in her one good eye answered his question. "I reckon that settles it. There ought to be a doctor in this burg. I'm getting you checked over."

"I don't need to see a doctor," she argued, although not very convincingly.

After talking to the hotel clerk Brazos discovered there were actually two doctors in town. The closest turned out to be only two blocks distance from the hotel. Doctor Harold Kerkman was a tall slim middle-aged man with an easy-going smile that immediately put Casey Sue at ease.

"My goodness," he exclaimed upon seeing her. With thumb and forefinger he gently tilted her chin up slightly to better examine her swollen cheek and bloodshot eye. "What in the world happened to you?" he said.

"I reckon some hombre shore worked me over," she replied trying to appear unruffled by the sight she must make.

"Yes, I can see that," Doctor Kerkman acknowledged under his breath. "How old are you, son?" he asked as he slowly waved a light back and forth in front of her eyes.

"Doctor, I—I'm not a—"

"Not a what?" he said gently when she hesitated, his shrewd gaze assessing her.

"A—boy," she said softly.

"I see. And that *hombre* you spoke of wouldn't be the cowboy waiting in the next room?"

"Oh, no, Doctor," she quickly denied. "If it hadn't of been for Brazos Kincaid, I don't know what would have happened to me."

"Hmm," he murmured. "Well, young lady I suppose it's none of my business, but you can't be more than a child."

"I'm older than I look," she smiled, her swollen cheek, however, making the undertaking more of a grimace.

"And that is…?" he prompted.

"I'm nineteen."

"Ah," he nodded. "May I inquire as to your name?"

"Casey Sue Thornton."

"Well, Miss Thornton you're fortunate; there's no evidence you suffered a concussion," he said feeling the back of her head behind her right ear. "In the meantime I'm going to give you something for that headache, and I suggest you don't do anything strenuous for a while."

After pouring a small amount of brown powder into a glass of water he handed the glass to her. "Here, drink this, it will relieve your discomfort."

Walking Casey Sue out of the room he approached the waiting Brazos. "Miss Thornton needs to take it easy for a while, and she shouldn't be allowed to fall into a deep sleep as there is still a danger of a concussion," he said.

Brazos nodded. "I'll see to her," he replied.

By the time they reached the hotel Casey Sue was feeling much better. The powder the doctor had given her had certainly done the trick she realized. While Brazos paid for another night's stay she went up to her room where she sat gingerly on the bed. She wanted nothing better to do than lay back on the soft mattress and sleep, but she knew she should heed the doctor's warning. There came a soft knock on the door.

"It's me, Brazos."

He opened the door and stepped inside before she could respond. His eyes searched hers and she saw the worry and anxiety in his, which despite her previous warning to watch her heart where this cowboy was concerned, warmed her.

"My headache is much better," she said answering his unspoken question.

"I reckon that's shore good to hear," he replied letting out a relieved sigh. He settled down in one of the chairs at the small table. We'll stay another day or two and rest up."

She didn't argue. Not immediately.

"What if he comes back—breaks in my room again?!" she shivered.

"I reckon I'll drag the mattress from the room next door and sleep here in your room. He'll have to get past me—What?" Brazos demanded as she stared skeptically at him. "It won't be no different than us spending the night together on the trail."

"Hah! That was before you discovered I was a girl," she patently pointed out.

"Yeah, well," he said, and she could swear his cheeks reddened. "Damn it, Case, we're pards, remember? I reckon I ain't gonna let you out of my sight. I'll keep you safe from them hombres. Trust me."

Trust him?! *'Humph,'* she wanted to say, *'who's going to keep me safe from you?'* She was aware first hand of his amorous liaisons to know not to trust Brazos Kincaid…not with her heart! She was determined above all not to fall for his easy charm. No matter how tempting. But she also knew she didn't want to be alone in that room, no more than she wanted to hit the trail so soon, not as sore and aching as she was… so…trust him she supposed she'd have to do.

Brazos pulled a deck of cards from his vest pocket and began to shuffle. He looked up at Casey Sue.

"I don't reckon you play?" he asked.

They had several hours to kill before returning to see the doctor, and having her fall asleep wasn't an option, not with the danger of her having suffered a concussion. He didn't want her to fall asleep and not wake up.

Casey Sue glanced over at the table. "I know how, if that's what you're asking," she said.

"Oh, yeah?" he grinned.

"Shore, being around a cow camp, I reckon you couldn't help knowing."

"What'll it be, Five card stud?" he drawled. "That is if you feel up to it."

"Shore," she said and joined him at the table. "What're we going to use as chips?"

"Aw, I don't reckon it would be sporting of me to take your money," he grinned, rather smugly she thought. "I got it," he said snapping his fingers. He pushed back his chair stood up and strode over to his pack where he extracted a box of bullets. He pushed the deck over in front of her. "Deal," he instructed, "while I divide these up."

Casey Sue gathered up the deck and began to shuffle with the skill of a cardsharp. Brazos halted what he was doing, staring.

"Where'd you learn to deal like that?" he demanded, mesmerized by her deft handling of the cards.

"Abe Brasee, my old boss. Did I tell you he was a Louisiana Creole gambler before he came to Texas?"

"Ah-huh," he grunted and started counting out the bullets again when out of the corner of his eye he watched her finishing the deal. And spied something he would have never suspect in a million years—not from this wisp of a girl. While her fingers moved skillfully as she dealt, making the cards fly across the table, he realized that their whirling flight distracted anyone from discerning that she could pluck a card from anywhere in the deck. And when he picked up the cards she had just dealt him it confirmed his suspicions. The little scamp was cheating like a professional. He shook his head slightly, and when he looked up at her, her eyes widened in recognition, and she grinned impishly.

CHAPTER SEVEN

Brazos and Casey Sue left Linrock two mornings later after getting the okay from the doctor. They purchased a pack horse and extra canvas water bags and otherwise replenishing their shrunken supplies at the general store down the street from the hotel. Once out of town they turned west on a narrow grass-grown trail that the clerk at the general store said would head them in the direction of Guadalupe. Several times during the day Brazos cast keen looks back over his shoulder watching for sign of anyone trailing them. He saw none, though he couldn't shake the feeling that someone was back there shadowing them.

"Do you reckon we're being followed," Casey Sue asked glancing back the way they had come.

"Like as not," Brazos shrugged, lips in a grim line.

She took a deep breath, nodded resolutely.

The land changed subtly the trail winding between low brush-covered foothills spotted, partly desert with long, bright lines of dry stream beds, which afforded little cover, to arroyos and gullies lined with mesquite, cottonwood and scrub-oak. Snow-covered mountains were seen in the far distance. Near evening the country appeared to be flattening out, greener in the open spaces though the cedar dotted bluffs stood up here and there. They halted at the mouth of a little canyon with grass and water and made camp. Unsaddling his horse, Brazos went to help Casey Sue. She gave him a strange look as he drug her saddle off under a cottonwood. He reached and untied her bedroll.

"Have a seat, Case and I'll have a fire going in a jiffy," he said. "Then I'll rustle up some grub."

"Brazos Kincaid, I ain't helpless," she exclaimed. "I been doing camp chores all by myself off and on since I left Louisiana six years ago with Paw and Uncle Will, and not to mention for the last three weeks ever since we—been riding together."

"Yeah, well, that was 'fore I found out you was a girl. Besides, that hombre gave you a good whop to your head. You just take it easy."

"That's awfully good of you, Brazos, but please, wait till I drop, will you?" she snorted and set about starting a fire.

Brazos prided himself on being a light sleeper, and tonight he counted on it. He had picked this little canyon for its seclusion. Sheltered like it was their campfire would be difficult to see unless one happened to ride up on them which would be hard for them to do without Brazos hearing or seeing them.

The moon rose and cast deep shadows along the canyon floor as he rolled a cigarette lighting the smoke with a twig from the fire. He eyed the little sleeping form a short distance away. Here on this venture, he was answering to a call that had now directed his movements—his life as had no other time. And it was one that neither logic nor intelligence could take stock of. The hold this little waif of a girl had on him was unyielding. He could never see a time when she would not be a part of his life. Finishing the cigarette, he dragged saddle, blankets and slicker under a thick bushy cedar, and made his bed there.

Brazos woke with a start. He lay unmoving listening. The night was quiet. A soft wind rustled the branches overhead. The sound came from where Casey Sue lay. She rolled restlessly in her bed emitting soft murmurings. She was dreaming. Suddenly she flailed with her arms uttering a moan of anguish. He thought she would wake herself, but her moaning only became louder. He rolled from his blankets and knelt beside her.

"Case, wake up!" he hissed shaking her.

She screamed and her flailing fist collided with his jaw before he managed to subdue her thrashing arms.

"Case, it's me, damn it."

"Brazos! Oh!" and she flung her arms about his neck. "He was there i-in my room. I couldn't f-fight him off—"

"It was just a dream, Case. You're safe. No body's gonna hurt you, ever again."

"Promise?" she said with shaky voice.

"Shore, pard. I promise."

She pulled away, gazed into his eyes. "I woke you. I'm sorry."

"I'm a light sleeper. It don't take much to wake me. Go back to sleep."

"I don't know if I can," she said shivering. "It was so real."

"I'll be close by," he assured her.

Brazos sat next to her for a long while listening, knowing finally by her soft even breathing that she had at last fallen asleep again. The hum of insects and the far away lament of coyotes once again became unbroken. He returned to his bed roll and stretched out. But sleep did not return quickly. The feel of strong, lissome, quivering arms, of dark tragic, intent eyes, held him firmly ensnared.

Brazos rose early the next morning and started the fire whereupon he put the coffee pot on to boil. Casey Sue stirred and sat upright on her bedroll. She hadn't slept well accounting it to her dark dream. For a moment she sat there as the tender fingers of dawn outlined the tiny black shapes of pine trees far above on top of the mountains.

After they finished their breakfast Brazos set down to consult the map that her uncle had given Case pin-pointing the location of the gold strike. It was quite detailed and Brazos could understand why her uncle was leery that someone would steal it. Brazos set about putting some of the landmarks to memory.

"What's this?" he suddenly queried pointing to writing on the space near the bottom of the map.

Casey Sue glanced over his shoulder, smiled. "That's Louisiana Creole."

"Oh, yeah? That's some kind of language?"

"Of course. I practically grew up speaking that as well as English."

"What's it say?"

"I'm not sure—"

"I thought you said you grew up speaking it."

"Oh, I know what it says, I just don't quite understand what Uncle Will meant by it," she replied frowning.

"Read it."

"Well, Uncle Will writes; *'Mon petit'*—that's his pet name for me," she said smiling wistfully—"*'écouter gardé'*—listen carefully—but this next part is what I don't follow. I'm thinking maybe it's just some random writing and has nothing to do with the map," she said.

"Go on, read what it says," Brazos directed, waiting as she translated her uncle's words into English.

"*'Three past the mule, look to the sunset.'*"

"Well I'll be. Seems like your uncle was being overly cautious in case this map fell into the wrong hands," Brazos said.

"Ah, that makes sense," she nodded. "The "mule" must be some kind of landmark."

"That's what I figure," he mused, "Looks like this map doesn't take us all the way to your uncle's gold strike."

"So what do we do?" she asked.

"Well, I reckon when we get to the end of this map, we'll just have to locate this "mule" and go from there."

Casey Sue opened her pack and extracted a small compact mirror and the case with her stage makeup. And taking a seat cross-legged on the ground began to apply the counterfeit mustache and fuzzy beard. She was aware of Brazos watching her.

"What?" she inquired innocuously glancing at his reflection in the tiny mirror.

"I reckon that fake beard an' all shore helps, but you're too dog-gone pretty, and with them long dark eyelashes, you ain't gonna fool no body," he snorted.

"I fooled you."

"Did not. I knew you was a girl all the time."

"Hah! You're a big liar, Brazos Kincaid," she snickered watching him in the mirror as he got abruptly to his feet and walked away.

'So, he thinks me pretty.' And she couldn't help grinning as she finished her makeup and stowed the mirror and other items back in her pack.

Still worried about being followed Brazos made a concerted effort to covering their tracks sticking to grassy places and hard ground. Anyone following them would not have an easy go of it. Casey Sue rode behind him and glancing back at her he smiled reassuringly. She smiled shyly back at him. The swelling in her cheek had receded and the black and purple bruise was fading rapidly.

The morning air was growing hot. For miles now there had been sparse vegetation. The valley floor at times broke into red hummocks, each one crowned with the delicate green leaves and lethal thorns of mesquite bushes. Yuccas grew in groves along with thickets of sturdy greasewood. Long inclines of tall grass-covered foothills rose to the knees of the mountains where acres of prickly pear and rabbit brush grew. It was a harsh and forbidding country, Brazos decided. And the foreboding feeling that they were being followed grew.

Nearing noon when the heat of the day began to oppress and hunger and thirst made themselves manifest, they halted in a grove of scrub oak which afforded some cover. Skirting the trees the trail led into a road which was hard packed and smooth from the tracks of cattle, stolen cattle Brazos reckoned figuring they had come across one of the roads used by border raiders. Twisting in his saddle Brazos took a long hard look back along their trail.

"Uh-huh!" he suddenly muttered.

"What is it?" Casey Sue exclaimed peering as he did back the way they had come.

"At least one rider, probably a mile back. He's mounted on a tall buckskin."

"I don't see anyone," Casey Sue murmured.

"I reckon he's back there. Shore wish I had bought a pair of binoculars at that general store," he grunted his narrow gaze fixed on a spot in the distance. Then he turned and peered at her. "I reckon this is as good a place as any," he said. "It's time we found out who that hombre is. See that stand of cottonwoods yonder..." he continued pointing.

She nodded.

"Follow this arroyo keeping out of sight," he instructed stepping from the saddle pulling his rifle from its scabbard as he did so. He tossed the reins to her "Take my horse and the pack horse with you and wait in them trees—"

"What are you going to do?" she demanded.

"I got a plan. I reckon I'm going to brace that hombre—"

"Oh, no, you're not leaving me behind!"

"Will you do as I say?!" he growled. "I don't want the horses to give me away. I'm going to bushwhack him."

"What if there's more than one rider back there?" she challenged.

"I reckon there's only one, and I intend to get the drop on him."

She glowered at him a moment, then with a huff started off leading the two horses. When she reached the stand of cottonwoods she slipped from the saddle and led the horses to the far side where she tied them. Clutching her Winchester she crept back to the edge of the trees where she could see the grove of scrub oak. Brazos was no longer in sight. Hunkering down she waited not taking her eyes from the place she had last seen Brazos.

Brazos watched the rider approach. Once or twice the man shot a long glance back over his shoulder. He was small and wiry with a coarse bronze face, slouchy of attire, and armed to the teeth mounted on a fine buckskin…and downright familiar. Brazos stepped from the covert in which he was crouched rifle leveled.

"Billy Joe Mercer," he called out.

The rider jerked his horse to a halt, hand dropping to the Colt at his hip, but then froze as his eyes took in the rifle in Brazos' hands, and then he darted a look up at Brazos' face.

"Brazos Kincaid?!" he hissed. "Hells fire! Yu 'bout skerd the pants off me," and his brown eyes, once tense and fidgety, visibly relaxed. He looked down at the rifle pointed at him. "Well, now is thet anyway te greet yur old pard?" he laughed loudly.

"We never was partners," Brazos said easily.

"Well, now, thet don't seem right do it? Why, we shore had a thing goin' there fer a while yu got te admit." He laughed again looking Brazos up and down. "Shore, I never figured I'd ever see the likes of yu this fer west of the Pecos."

"I reckon more like you didn't figure on ever seeing me again," Brazos declared menacingly.

"Aw, now, yu ain't holdin' thet little episode with Goodman agin me are yu? Shore, there weren't no way I could have sprung yu from thet lynchin' party," Mercer said his brown eyes blinking disarmingly.

Brazos eyed him a moment in silence. "I reckon not, but I'm not forgetting who steered me up that canyon—"

"Aw, how the hell was I te know Goodman an' his bunch was moseyin' around up there!" Mercer avowed his brown eyes wide with the innocence of a lamb. "Besides, with yur rep with a gun I shore figured yu'd be up te handlin' any trouble thet might come along," Mercer continued.

Brazos was silent studying the man who imparted an inauspicious shrug and then darted a look back over his shoulder.

"You expecting company?" Brazos asked.

Mercer shrugged sheepishly shifting in his saddle then his face brightened. "Say Brazos, I reckon it's shore good te see yu."

"Is that so?" Brazos snorted.

"It shore is," Mercer went on. "Yu know I never was much on this lone-wolf dodging, though I've shore 'nough done it of late out of necessity. Give me a pardner any day."

"I don't reckon we're suited," Brazos said.

"I beg te differ," Mercer grinned. "Why, with yur rep with a gun an' my knowhow, we could be rollin' in clover."

"On the underside looking up, you mean," Brazos scoffed.

"Hah! Yu know what yur trouble is Kincaid? Yu're too persnickety," Mercer jeered. "Here, I bet yu don't have more'n a few pesos te yur name."

"I got plans," Brazos replied tipping his sombrero back off his forehead with his thumb.

"Oh, yeah? Let me guess—"

But before Mercer could complete his retort there came the ping of a bullet ricocheting off the trunk of a scrub oak near Mercer's head followed by the distant crack of a rifle.

"Fork yur horse, Brazos!" Mercer shouted, but before he could set spurs to his buckskin, Brazos grabbed hold of his bridle. "Let go!" Mercer ordered.

"My horse is yonder in them trees," Brazos said nodding in the direction of the cottonwoods.

"Well, damn it, climb aboard," Mercer yelled kicking a stirrup free.

Plunging his booted foot in the empty stirrup, Brazos swung up behind Mercer and they bound off, the added weight seeming of little consequence to the big buckskin. Brazos glanced back over his shoulder and saw a cloud of dust down the road in the direction Mercer had come probably a little more than a quarter mile away. He counted six riders. They were half way to the trees when another shot rang out and Brazos heard the bullet whiz close by his ear.

"What the hell did you do to get them riders so riled up?" Brazos yelled.

"No time te explain now," Mercer shouted back over his shoulder.

Casey Sue, hunkering down in the stand of cottonwoods stared intently at Brazos and the rider on the tall buckskin. They seem to be having an almost friendly chat, though the man kept glancing back every little bit over his shoulder the way he had come. What was that all about? she wondered. But then suddenly she heard the rifle shot and saw the group of riders break into the open a half mile back. Casey Sue's heart caught in her throat. The rider on the buckskin looked as though he was going to spur away and leave Brazos, but that worthy grabbed the buckskin's bridle. A moment later Brazos leaped up behind the rider and the horse bound off racing toward the trees where she crouched.

Casey Sue ran to where the horses were tied and freeing them swung into the saddle of her big black. With Brazos' roan and the packhorse in tow she spurred her horse out from the cover of the trees, keeping the horses at a swift stride. She looked back at the big buckskin thundering toward her and spurred her black faster, Brazos' roan and the pack horse pounding behind. As the big buckskin came alongside Brazos' horse which had surged ahead coming abreast of Casey Sue's black, Brazos leaped onto the roan's back without breaking rhythm and Casey Sue tossed him the reins.

CHAPTER EIGHT

asey Sue flung Brazos a searching look as if to say, *'what in hell is going on?'* Brazos shook his head and eased his horse back alongside the packhorse that was dragging back on his halter rope not liking the rapid pace. He untied his lariat rope and whirring out a loop gave the packhorse's rump a hard whack. Snorting and with ears laid back the horse bound forward coming alongside Casey Sue's black. A moment later Brazos hurried a look back over his shoulder and was relieved to see the riders pursuing them had fallen back.

"No hosses in thet bunch to worry us," Mercer called out.

Brazos had the same conviction. By the looks of their lathered mounts, they weren't about to overtake them. Nearing sunset they reached the mouth of a wide gorge with steep tree-covered slopes on each side. A narrow stream cut through the middle of the canyon. All four horses were winded and lashed with sweat and lather. Mercer turned and started up the canyon splashing through the water. Brazos and Casey Sue followed without comment. After some distance up the canyon following its twisting course through the knee-deep stream they arrived at a point where the canyon floor below was no longer visible and a smaller canyon branched off to the right. It was here Mercer halted, and leaning a forearm on his saddle horn turned his dancing brown eyes upon his two companions.

"I reckon we're safe now," he grinned.

"Who were them fellers?" Brazos asked, shoving his sombrero back off his forehead with his thumb. "And what're they after you for?"

"Ah, just a little misunderstandin' back at Guadalupe," he shrugged.

"What do you mean?" Brazos retorted giving him a penetrating look.

"Wal, I reckon they took exception te me borrowin' a few pesos from their e'lustrous bank—"

"You robbed the bank?!"

"Wal, heck yeah. Since they wasn't 'bout te give me no loan, an' I kinda needed some necessities."

"You robbed a bank?! Are you loco?!"

"I don't reckon it's thet big a deal," Mercer guffawed with a dismissive wave. "I don't know why they got so upset. I only made off with four hundred bucks. They shore got plenty more te spare."

"It shore the hell is a big deal!" Brazos shouted. "Now that posse's got me and my partner pegged as part of your gang!"

"Well, now thet yu put it thet way, I reckon yu might be right. Wal, there ain't nothin' te do but hide out until things cool down."

"Brazos! My uncle. We can't—" Casey Sue said easing her horse up next to Brazos.

"Just for a day or two, Case, until we make shore that posse's not on to us," he replied in the same low voice.

"Wal, Brazos, who's this young feller?" Mercer asked directing a not unfriendly eye at Casey Sue.

"Billy Joe, meet my pard, Case Thornton," Brazos said. "Case, pard, this here is Billy Joe Mercer, an old acquaintance."

"Old acquaintance?" Mercer snorted. "I reckon Brazos hyar has shore a short memory seein' as how we was pards once not thet long onwards."

"No sense in bringing that up," Brazos said curtly. "If it weren't for Case here that necktie party yu run off an' abandoned me to would have shore swung me up."

"Aw, I reckon yu ain't gonna let me off the hook fer thet, huh?" Mercer grumbled.

"I reckon not, Billy Joe," Brazos replied.

It was late afternoon. For the last three hours they had been following Billy Joe Mercer, climbing the roughest and most difficult trail that Brazos had ever seen. He kept glancing back over his shoulder at Casey Sue bringing up the rear behind the packhorse he led. At each worried look, she gave him a resilient smile, but he could see the growing weariness in her eyes. The ascent was slow; having to go around rocks and in some cases fallen trees lying long dead across the path.

Abruptly Mercer left the stream and nudging his horse up a shallow rise to where the trail broke out upon a large plateau. Brazos reined up and Casey Sue came alongside. Brazos estimated they must have climbed a thousand feet or more from the valley floor to reach this elevation. They both took in the sight before them. Horses and cattle grazed freely and a number of crude log cabins, some with smoke curling lazily upward from makeshift mud chimneys, squatted beneath the tall pines at the edge of the forest. Farther on they saw other cabins of likewise log construction surrounded by tall pines. Standing in the shade beneath the porch attached to a house bigger than the others was a white woman. She appeared young and pretty. She eyed them curiously. Brazos saw two or three other women who looked Mexican and a number of white men who appeared to be doing nothing while several Mexicans worked in a field some distance beyond.

"What is this place?" Brazos queried.

"Platt's Peak," Mercer said, twisting in his saddle to peer back at him. "Come along, I'll introduce yu te Platt."

"Platt, huh," Brazos said.

"Yep, ain't heard him called by no other handle."

Brazos and Casey Sue fell in behind Mercer as he started off. The trail widened and opened upon a kind of square lined by more adobe and log buildings of rudest construction. Dogs lay in the shade of the houses and big-eyed Mexican children stared from several open doorways as they rode past. Lolling on benches before a long, low log structure, which evidently served as a store and saloon were several white men in rough garb. As Brazos and Casey Sue approached following Mercer one of the loungers stood.

"Bust me, Billy Joe's back! Who's that with yu, Billy?" the man demanded. The others eyed the new comers with only moderate interest.

At that juncture several men crowded out of the door, and stood listening to the exchange.

"Wess, meet my old pard, Brazos Kincaid," Mercer said easily. "An' this youngster is Case Thornton."

The man called Wess nodded giving Brazos a long keen stare.

A tall man of stalwart physique, one of those who had been listening by the door stepped forward. His manner proclaimed him a leader.

"I'm Platt," the man said authoritatively. He had a long face, a thick dark beard, and clear cold blue eyes.

"Mercer, have yu brung me two recruits," he demanded, though his gaze was fixed in close scrutiny upon Brazos. He wasn't a Texan. In fact Brazos did not recognize even one of these outlaws—for in truth that's what they were—as native to his state.

Brazos looked at Platt aware of Casey Sue edging her big black closer to his side and Mercer's narrow, curious gaze upon him.

"Sorry, Platt, I don't reckon he has," Brazos said. "Me and my pard just need a day or two to rest up, then we'll be on our way."

"So you're in trouble and had te go on the dodge, huh? What kind of trouble?" Platt questioned. He seemed eager, curious, speculative.

"Platt, yu know who this is?" Mercer asked in a loud voice. "This hyar feller happens te be Brazos Kincaid," he said jerking his chin at Brazos.

"Brazos Kincaid—" Wess exhaled his inhospitable bearing rapidly altering. "Air yu *thet* Brazos Kincaid?"

"Yu bet yore saddle he's *thet* Brazos Kincaid," Mercer exclaimed. "Back in Texas we was pards."

Brazos shot a look at Mercer.

"Gunslinger, huh?" Platt said.

Brazos let his silence answer for him.

"Wal, meet my top man, Chess Lovelace. I reckon yu've heard of him," Platt said, pointing with a jerk of his thumb to the tall slender man at his side.

A thick black mustache drooped over the outlaw's lower lip in a face strikingly pale. His black hair was long and hung loose about his shoulders. He stared at Brazos with cold calculating eyes.

"Chess Lovelace?" Brazos said coolly. "Naw, I don't reckon I have."

Lovelace's eyes narrowed to slits, but he said nothing.

This would never do, Casey Sue fumed to herself as she fell in beside Brazos following Mercer. No it wouldn't do at all. This was an outlaw hideout for goodness sakes! What would happen if these men found out she was a girl? She couldn't hide the fact very long in these surroundings. Mercer led them down the road to a tiny adobe shack partially hidden in a stand of trees.

"The place ain't big, but make yoreselves at home," Mercer said dismounting and leading his horse into an open shed.

Brazos swung to the ground and after a moment's hesitation Casey Sue followed. The shack had two rooms. There was one window in each, without any coverings, and bare floors. One room contained blankets, weapons, saddles, and bridles; the other a stone fireplace, a rude table and two bunks on opposite sides of the small room. There was a scarred and chipped cupboard and a number of blackened utensils. Casey Sue caught Brazos' arm not venturing any further into the shack.

"Brazos, we—I can't stay here in this shack—this camp," she hissed in a low voice.

"I know, Case. I'll get us out of this, don't worry," he whispered in return.

She glowered at him.

"Say, Billy that's right good of you, but we'll just throw our bedrolls back in the woods a bit," Brazos said.

"No need. I got me a little señorita I'm sparkin'," Mercer returned slyly with a bold wink. "So I reckon yu two can bed down hyar fer as long as yu figure on hangin' around. I'll come by tomorrow an' clear out my gear so as yu'll have more room."

"I reckon we won't be staying long," Brazos said.

"Tellin' Platt thet yu wouldn't join his gang ain't gonna make him take a likin' to yu," Mercer said eyes shifting from Brazos to Casey Sue and back.

"I'd remind you Billy, you led us up here."

"Yeah, I reckon thet weren't good thinkin' on my part," he admitted and walked out.

Brazos glanced at Casey Sue. "I'll see to the horses and bring in our packs. How about you start a fire?"

Casey Sue nodded and made a face as she hesitantly glanced around. They were in the middle of an outlaw camp, and there wasn't even a cover over the windows. She eyed the two bunks, one on each side of the small room.

"I don't reckon it's any different than sleeping on the trail," she muttered to herself. "We've been doing that for days."

She bit her lower lip. They had been together now sleeping under the stars for days, and sometimes within inches of one another much closer than the ten feet that separated the two bunks. But for some reason it just seemed different. Maybe it was because on the trail there was a wide sweeping sky above them and open spaces all around. Here inside this small shack…it just wasn't the same.

She went into the other room containing saddles, bridles, a box of tools, and several blankets piled haphazardly against one wall. Rummaging about in the tool box she found horseshoe nails and a hammer. Snatching up a horse blanket from one of the saddles, she retraced her steps and draped the blanket over the window, securing it with horseshoe nails effectively preventing anyone from peering in.

Satisfied, she returned to the other room and taking a lariat rope she found coiled over the saddle horn of one of the saddles she returned. After pounding nails into each adjacent wall she strung the rope across one corner of the room and taking two blankets hung them over the rope and using nails like straight pins fastened them thereby closing off one corner and the bed from the rest of the room. She stood back and surveyed her work. It would do. She trusted Brazos, but after all, a girl needed a little privacy. She bent and set to work building a fire in the hearth.

"Well, looks like you've settled in."

Casey Sue glanced back over her shoulder to see Brazos standing in the doorway.

"I decided to make the best of it," she replied turning back to the fire.

Casey Sue lay on her bunk behind her curtain of blankets staring up at the rough ceiling beams. It was stuffy inside her sanctuary and she had opened the window a few inches. From somewhere not far distant the soft strumming of a guitar drifted through the narrow opening. Then from farther away the sound of a woman's lusty laugh followed by voices raised in argument. Casey Sue took a deep breath fully expecting to hear the crack of gunshots, but none came and the querulous voices quieted. She listened to Brazos' relaxed breathing from the other side of the small room. He didn't appear bothered by the fact they were in the middle of an outlaw camp. Indeed he seemed quite unperturbed by their situation, remembering how he had gone out and returned later with two heaping plates of Mexican food; beans, rice, beef and large mugs of coffee that he had acquired from somewhere—probably from some sultry-eyed young señorita, which there seemed to be an abundance of in this outlaw camp. Or maybe the pretty young white woman she remembered seeing in front of the big house, fixed the food for him. That would be like him. And the fact that that irritated her only made her annoyance the more acrimonious. Nevertheless, she had eaten every bite on her plate. It had been delicious, not to mention she had been starving.

Brazos lay there making an effort to quietly breathe feigning sleep. But he wasn't asleep. He was wide awake and he was doing some deep thinking about Casey Sue. When had he started thinking of her as Casey Sue? The last week or so, he realized. Once he had discovered her secret it was impossible to see her as anything but a beautiful young woman. Or so he imagined every male who set eyes on her would guess immediately. He traced his thoughts back over their arrival at the hideout. He sought out each face in his mind, especially the outlaw boss, Platt, but couldn't recall the slightest inkling in their eyes or manner that they might have taken notice of Casey Sue in any aspect other than a young boy.

He smiled in the dark. He had to admit she had perfected her disguise; the way she swung her shoulders with the sort of swagger so like a boy when she walked. Her bold glances, the way she sat on her haunches one knee higher than the other in cowboy fashion, how when she stood she brashly hitched up her belt settling the big gun comfortably on her hip. She said that she rode with a trail driving outfit. She obviously had time to observe and practice her skill pretending to be a boy. And, of course, the fuzzy beard she glued on her upper lip and chin put the final touches on her masquerade. But that didn't assuage his concern. He had to get her away from this place. There was too much that could go wrong…besides, he had made a promise to help her, keep her safe until she found her uncle's gold claim. Well, he would get them out of this jamb he had gotten them into.

CHAPTER NINE

The next morning Brazos was awake and dressed before Casey Sue stirred from her sanctuary behind the makeshift wall of blankets. He had breakfast ready, fresh bread, eggs and beef steaks he procured from a Mexican woman at a nearby hut. When Casey Sue made her appearance he could tell she had been up for a while and had affixed her fake theatre mustache and beard. They sat at the little table. Casey Sue was quiet as they ate and he could sense her impatience. She wanted to leave here. So did he, for that matter, but it might be better to wait a day just to make certain they didn't run into Mercer's posse. He voiced his concern. She didn't argue but he knew she differed. It was there in the flash of her blue eyes.

"How about we have a look-see around this place?" he said which brightened her. "So they'll know we're not hiding. But stay close to me."

"Don't worry," she retorted hitching up her gun belt pointedly.

Mercer's little shack sat against the first rise of the slope of trees and by climbing a few steps they had a good view of the area and the valley below. The mountaintop hideout was an ideal outlaw retreat. The narrow trail up was easily defended against almost any number of men coming up the rocky path—if they could even find it. He was stumped however as to how they got supplies in, and in any quantity up to the hideout. And secondly, how did they prosper? From what he could see the outlaws were well fed and had money to spend.

They hadn't gone too far when they met Billy Joe Mercer. He didn't appear to see them as he walked along head down, hands stuffed in his pockets. Brazos called out to him.

"Huh?" he exclaimed glancing up as though surprised out of deep thought. His normally carefree visage held a grim expression. He looked from Brazos to Casey Sue, and then heaved a long frustrated sigh.

"What's the matter?" Brazos queried.

"Aw hell! I reckon I shore been skinned, pard," he said.

"How's that?"

"I reckon it's my own damn fault lettin' myself get joshed inte playin' cards with that cheatin' no good—" He broke off amid a string of cusses.

"How much did you lose?"

"Everything!" Mercer snapped. "All my cash—"

"All *your* cash, huh? That wouldn't be the money from that bank caper you pulled?" Brazos drawled pointedly.

Mercer shot him a sheepish look. "Wal, yeah, I reckon," he grunted. "Say, have yu've ate?"

Brazos nodded.

"Yeah, there's shore one consolin' fact round this here camp," Mercer said. "Plenty of good juicy beef te eat. An' it don't cost a short bit."

"I reckon that's Platt's game, huh, rustling?"

Mercer nodded. "I should smile. Not just rustlin' like yu an' me know, but big time. Platt has several small camps up an' down the river."

"The river?"

"Rio Grande."

At Brazos' puzzled look, Mercer smirked. "Shore yu're turned around with all thet backtrackin' up the trail. Come on," he motioned with his chin for Brazos and Casey Sue to follow him.

They passed a good many Mexicans, some tending small farm plots, others lolling about, while still others, mostly older women, busy with various tasks. Children ran about freely. Mercer led them to the south side of the camp where they could see down a rather steep but winding wagon road to crude docks jutting out into the river. Several enormous flat-bottom boats were moored along the river bank.

"That's the Rio Grande?" Brazos said realizing access to Mexico was easy and quick down the trail opposite leading to the Rio Grande which rolled away between high bluffs.

"Yep. 'cross yonder is Mexico—" Mercer nodded and looked off down the slope. "I reckon I'll go clear muy things out of the shack." And without another word he walked back the way they had come.

"I reckon Billy Joe cleared up something that was puzzling me," Brazos said in a low voice.

"What do you mean?" she asked peering up at him from under the brim of her floppy black hat.

"Well," he mused. "I was wondering how Platt got his supplies up here on this mountain, but Billy Joe solved that mystery when he showed us the wagon road down to the river. It ain't hard to follow that them big flat-bottom boats would shore be good for hauling cattle on the hoof—rustled cattle that he floats down the river into Mexico where he sells them for a fair profit. And it's a shore bet them boats don't leave any tracks."

"Ah," Casey Sue nodded understandingly.

When they entered Mercer's old shack they discovered that none of Billy Joe's gear had been removed.

"Brazos," Casey Sue said worriedly, "Platt shore has got this rustling business well organized. We got to get away from this place."

"I know, Case. We'll leave in the morning."

Brazos stepped into the other room and halted hand hovering over his gun. A man sat in one of the chairs before the table. Brazos couldn't tell his height, but he gave the impression of being tall and slender. He was bronze of face the result of long exposure to the outdoors. A thick black mustache drooped over his upper lip. It matched the dark hair that showed below his wide-brimmed sombrero. His piercing eyes, black as his mustache, surveyed Brazos with keen interest.

"I shore would feel a mite better if yu'd relax that gun hand," the man said smiling disarmingly. He sat with both hands palm-flat on the table.

"Who are you?" Brazos drawled.

"I reckon I'm known here 'bouts as Matt Jacobson," he replied in that easy drawl. "I happened to hear yu tellin' yur partner thet yu plan to leave Platt's Peak in the mornin'."

"So you did," Brazos said.

"Don't wait 'til mornin'. Go while it's dark. By mornin' it'll be too late."

"Meaning?" Brazos replied softly.

"There's been considerable talk in camp about your throwin' of a gun," Jacobson went on, "Luke Benson claims he seen yu draw once o'ver Big Springs, an' said he ain't seen yur equal. He said he was watchin' close but couldn't follow yur hand when yu drawed. Billy Joe Mercer allowed the same. That yu an' him were once old pards."

Brazos coolly studied Jacobson not saying a word.

"Platt's two cronies, Chess Lovelace an' Jeff Sibert, an' maybe Platt himself, shore didn't like the reference made about yur speed. An' some of the fellers allowed your draw might have been just an accident, but I reckon most of 'em figgered different—"

"You're shore doing a lot a talking, Jacobson," Brazos said aware that Casey Sue had stepped into the room and moved off to the side.

Jacobson's eyes flitted to her for a moment before shifting back to Brazos.

"Vivian—that's Platt's woman. She's quite a looker; I reckon yu couldn't help noticin' her, only white woman here." Jacobson's eyes flashed back to Casey Sue. "She swears yur pard there is a woman—"

Brazos heard Casey Sue's quick intake of breath.

"Platt scoffed it off, but I reckon it caught his attention," Jacobson continued. "That's why I'm advisin' yu to shuck this place 'fore mornin'."

"Ah-huh, Jacobson. Why are you telling us this?" Brazos drawled watching him keenly.

"Because…I need yur help."

"Is that a fact?" Brazos said eyeing him speculatively.

"Yu have a rep, Brazos Kincaid as a straight shooter, an' not just with yur gun. Yu're no criminal…yet. Throwin' a gun in self defense—that ain't no crime. Yu don't know me, granted, 'cause Matt Jacobson's not my real name—" He stared long and hard at Brazos. "An' I'm takin' a chance that what I've heard 'bout yu is true—takin' a chance an' trustin' with my life, as a matter of fact."

"Get on with it," Brazos pressed quietly. "What do you want from me?"

"Wal, I'm puttin' my life in yur hands, Brazos Kincaid, by what I'm 'bout te tell yu." He glanced at Casey Sue then back at Brazos, motioned them closer. "My name is William Hardie—Bill fer short," he said in a voice barely about a whisper. "I'm a Texas Ranger—"

That was the last thing Brazos expected the man to say—Texas Ranger! It didn't make sense and the expression on his face must have shown it. He heard Casey Sue's little gasp, but didn't take his eyes off Jacobson—or Hardie as he now called himself. Why was he telling them this? And what was a Texas Ranger doing in the middle of an outlaw hideout? And he realized at that instant what a chance the man had taken revealing himself to them.

"I've been workin' under cover fer months infiltratin' Platt's gang of rustlers, but I have a strong hunch that Platt suspects. That shifty-eyed, Sibert. We met once before several years ago, though I reckon he don't recall the incident…but he will, an' when it comes te him, my dodge is over."

As he talked he pulled a slip of paper wrapped in oilskin from a hidden compartment in his belt. He offered it to Brazos who unfastened the flap and saw that it was a paper identifying Hardie as a Texas Ranger. It carried the official Seal of the Texas Rangers, signed by a Colonel J. McNulty. Brazos handed it back to Hardie who quickly replaced it in his belt.

"Say, I reckon this is New Mexico territory. What business does the Texas Rangers have here?" Brazos queried.

"What yu say is shore true, but Pratt an' his gang do their rustlin' over east of the Pecos in Texas an' float the beefs down the river on barges te this here hideout. So I reckon it shore is Ranger business."

"What do want me to do?" Brazos asked.

"I've got te get a message te Captain McKinney; let him know the layout of this place. They need to know when they send in Rangers to arrest Platt and take down his band. Platt's watchin' me like a hawk. If I tried to slip away…Wal, that'd be the farm fer me."

"The wagon trail down to the river…that looks too easy," Brazos mused.

"Yeah, yu'd never get far that way."

"That leaves the path down the mountain…" Casey Sue said quietly.

"It'd be bad enough in the daylight, Case, but at night?" Brazos growled looking at Casey Sue. "It's too damn dangerous."

"We can do it, Brazos. Just let the horses have their head. They'll find the path down," she insisted determinedly.

"The little lady has the right of it," Hardie said. "If yu wait til daylight, it'll be too late."

"If it's that easy to slip out of here, why don't you do it? Why send us?" Brazos drawled.

Hardie nodded easily. "I reckon I could take that chance, but there's more to it than that. It's mighty significant fer me te be here when the boys bust in on Platt an' his gang," Hardie said and for an instant it seemed he was going to explain, but stopped himself.

"There's a troop of Rangers camped somewhere between here and Guadalupe waitin' fer word from me. It'd shore fire be my end if I tried to do it my own. So I'm hopin' yu'd get the message to Cap McKinney." He held out a folded paper. "It's in code, except the map ain't. So if Platt or his bunch stops yu, chew it and swallow it. *Comprende?*"

"I reckon I understand," Brazos said.

CHAPTER TEN

razos halted, waiting. He glanced back at Casey Sue sensing her anxiety although he could barely make out her dark form mounted on her black horse a few feet away. They had left one lamp lit in the little shack. The blanket over the window was drawn but Brazos saw a long, dark shadow cross the window. This would have deceived Brazos had he not been told by Hardie about his device for making shadows blow across the blanketed window to give the appearance of someone moving about inside. Lawless men of this class, Hardie explained, were sometimes exceedingly simple and gullible.

Without a word he started off leading his big roan up through the tall pines where the thick needles muted the sound of the horse's hoofs making a wide circuitous detour around the outlaw camp. Casey Sue followed trailing the packhorse her Winchester resting on her thighs. With thick shadows all around and the cold stars overhead, Brazos, sober in thought, worried as to what the end of this strange and fateful adventure would be. He had lead Casey Sue up here to this rustler hideout, and now her safety rested in his hands.

There was no trail and the night was so black that Brazos could see only patches of ground beneath the pines. Shadowy movement, the faint strumming of a guitar interrupted by the occasional boisterous laughter from the rustler camp was a comforting sound. At least no one appeared to be aware of their furtive flight. By and by mesquites and rocks began to appear making progress still harder but signaling they were nearing the canyon trail. Brazos, searching the darkness ahead, felt some sense of familiarity with things and realized they were probably near the start of the narrow trail down.

Across the valley on the far horizon lightning flashed. It seemed strange that no sounds accompanied the almost constant flares brightening the distant night sky. He went on until rocks and brush barred further progress, and then he backtracked coming suddenly upon what he recognized as the well-used trail. With a sigh of relief he stepped up to Casey Sue's horse.

"I think this is the trail," he whispered. "Keep close to me."

Her face was a pale oval beneath her black sombrero, but he saw her head dip in acknowledgement. He mounted and edged his horse to the lead, and then let him have his head trusting the big roan to find the easiest course down the steep trail. Slowly they worked their way downward, the creak of saddle leather, the occasional dull clack of iron hoofs on rock, the only sound. The descent was slow, though aided by the constant flashes of lightning which at times brightened the whole vicinity making it easier to navigate around rocks and in some cases fallen trees that Brazos recalled lying long dead across the path.

It seemed that the storm was moving closer as the hours passed with their progress much slower than the way up had been the day before. The only comfort was that they continued downward the horses slowly picking their way. Brazos guessed it was a few hours before dawn when the horses came upon the small stream leading out of the canyon. They had reached the bottom of the trail. Brazos heard Casey's sigh of relief as she edged her horse up beside him.

"Let the horses drink," he said voice low.

"Brazos, I been thinking," Casey Sue whispered. "Hardie said them Rangers were camped between here and Guadalupe."

"Yea, Case, I reckon he did, and you're thinking what I'm thinking. We're shore gonna run into that posse that was after Meeker if we head back to Guadalupe," declared Brazos. "Well, I don't reckon they got a good look at us, but they shore might recognize our horses, that black of yours is shore one in a million. We shore will be taking a chance, Case."

"Well, we can't let that Ranger Hardie down. I reckon he's depending on us," she said quietly.

"Then I reckon we head south," he said grimly.

"I'm just happy we're free of that outlaw camp," she sighed.

"Hands up! Texas Rangers!"

"They're up," Brazos called out.

The dark night hid the owner of the voice, but in the next distant flash of lightning Brazos caught the shadowy forms of at least a dozen riders and heard the muffled stomp of hoofs and the shuffling of movement from a grove of cedars several yards away. They must have been waiting silently in the dark, hearing their approach. Brazos cursed under his breath. He didn't like being caught flatfooted.

"Texas Rangers you say? Hey, is there a Captain McKinney in your bunch?" Brazos called.

"Who the hell air yu," came the reply out of the dark amid bright flashes of lightning.

"Name's Brazos Kincaid, and my partner Case Thornton," Brazos answered. "I reckon it's important I meet up with Captain McKinney."

"I'm McKinney," the unseen voice said. "Speak up."

"Well, I shore would like to take you on your word, Captain, but I reckon I'll shore need to see some identification."

There was a long moment of silence, and then the black shape of horse and rider materialized out the darkness slowly approaching. The rider halted several feet away.

"Brazos Kincaid, come forward alone, slowly, hands in the air."

The rider was curious but rightfully suspicious.

Brazos nudged the big roan into a walk, his gun hand raised. A few feet from the rider he halted. Lightning illuminated the black dome of the sky from one end to the other, one bright flash following after another. Brazos made out the rider's features. He had a not so young face beneath a black sombrero, cold and set in an almost ruthless guise. The man was apparently scrutinizing Brazos with the same intensity that Brazos was studying him. From far down the range low thunder rumbled.

"So yur Brazos Kincaid," the man grunted after a tense moment. Yu're some younger than I expected."

"Yes, sir," Brazos drawled in a voice that suggested humor.

The man reached a gloved hand and slowly turned the corner of his vest inside out. The next flash of lightning clearly showed the round badge encircling a five-pointed star in the center.

"I reckon you're who you say you are," Brazos drawled.

"Wal, what is it yu wanted te tell me?" McKinney asked.

Instead of answering immediately, Brazos handed over the message Ranger Hardie had given him.

"Bill Hardie asked me to see that you got this," he said.

"The hell yu say," McKinney snapped reaching to take the folded paper.

Not waiting for the next lightning flash, McKinney struck a match with his thumb and in the flare of its flame opened the paper.

"Men, come on up here," McKinney called, and at least ten riders, all in dark garb and heavily armed, reined up around McKinney. He struck another match. "Wal, its shore the hell from Bill, no mistakin' it. Let's go back yonder in them cedars and light a small fire. We got some plannin' te do. Come along Brazos and bring yore partner."

A small fire burned in the center of the cedar grove where the men gathered around as close as space permitted. Casey Sue squeezed in next to Brazos, a lone girl amid a dozen black-garbed Texas Rangers. The Ranger Captain McKinney laid out the map Hardie had made showing the layout of the outlaw camp.

"Reckon Brazos heah just come from the camp. Anything you can add?" McKinney asked, handing the map to Brazos who shook his head after a long glance at the exceptionally thorough drawing.

McKinney passed the map around so each man could study it.

"Wal, I reckon that map's a bonus, an' this heah storm is shore a windfall. It'll cover our movement. Brazos how tough a climb an' how long will it take us te get te the camp?"

"I reckon two, maybe three hours. Lots of twists and turns and rocks and down trees in the way," Brazos replied.

"Wal, men, check yore gear. We leave pronto," declared McKinney.

The men sprang into action. McKinney turned to Brazos. "Brazos Kincaid, yu're shore welcome te come along," he said.

"Shore I reckon, but me and my pard are on our way to the boy's ailing uncle and we shore lost a heap of time getting sidetracked like we did," he said and went on to explain how they had wound up at the outlaw camp.

"Meeker, huh? I know thet name," he mused, but said no more about the man. "Wal, no matter, it shore was lucky fer us thet yu did. I reckon we'd have been in a fix if yu hadn't found thet camp. We'd have never spotted the entrance te this canyon. An' Bill might not have been able te get word te us. Thanks my friend," he said and stuck out his hand.

Brazos clasped the hard calloused hand, but made no answering comment. A moment later Brazos and Casey Sue watched the dark riders disappear into the night. They stayed watching and listening until the sound of their movement was swallowed up by the darkness.

Lightning continued to flash in number and brilliance filling the heavens so that there was no defining point where one started and the other ended.

"Oh Brazos!" Casey Sue cried, face turned upward. "I've never seen the like. It's terribly scary and wondrous all at once!"

"It dang shore is. But I don't like it none at all," Brazos said huskily. "We need to find some shelter."

A soft rain began to fall and they donned their slickers, but the hard downpour that they expected did not come about and in the gray of dawn the storm had disappeared over the western mountains.

The makeup of the land had changed. Cottonwood and mesquite became less and less abundant replaced by cedar and some pine on the higher slopes. They saw cattle everywhere, though not in large herds. Near evening they descended the pine and spruce-timbered slope to enter a gully where water ran over rocks. Brazos let his horse pick his way along the rocky course of the rapidly moving stream. Casey Sue followed behind leading the pack horse. Mounting a slope beneath the tall pines, they reined to a halt. It was a beautiful white-grassed park, fringed by forest.

"I reckon we ought to make camp," Brazos said eyeing the sheltered park.

"It'll be cold beans and peaches," Casey Sue said, "Unless you think it's safe to light a fire."

"It's kind of sheltered here, and I shore could go for some hot coffee with them beans," Brazos remarked. "Then I reckon you ought to rest a spell, you've been swaying in your saddle."

She gave him a grateful look.

Supper concluded and the pans washed and put away, Casey Sue sought her bedroll. The loneliness and silence of the forest was comforting. The hoot of an owl came from somewhere high in the trees.

"Do you think they're still following us?" Casey Sue asked.

"Who, the posse?" Brazos queried.

"Naw, stickman and his partner."

"Hmm," he murmured. He hadn't forgotten the two, especially the big bearded hombre who had assaulted Casey Sue. It was obvious she hadn't either.

"I reckon so, Case," Brazos drawled. "Our little detour to that outlaw camp might have thrown them off some, but my guess is they're still on our trail. We best keep a close watch."

She nodded and lay back on her bedroll staring up through the trees.

The day broke beautifully with the sound of a mockingbird high in the branches of spruce. They looked out upon the gray-sloped snow-capped mountains to the east. Pure and white, remote and insurmountable, rose the glistening peaks high into the blue sky. While Casey Sue started breakfast, Brazos went to fetch the horses which he had hobbled the night before. On his return he smelled wood smoke and the savoy aroma of meat cooking. He smiled to himself. Case had set her snares out last night and he was about to taste the results—roast rabbit.

When they got underway the sun was cresting the high ridge. The land leveled out affording easy progress. Midafternoon Brazos suddenly came upon fresh horse tracks which brought him up short. He dismounted and hunkered down to study them. Six horses. It appeared they had crossed their path and then circled north in their same direction. Brazos felt a tremor race down his spine. An awful premonition assaulted him. He shook his head letting out his pent-up breath accounting it to no more than an attack of nerves.

"What's wrong?" Casey Sue cried.

He debated for an instant of not telling her, but decided to voice what had momentarily struck him.

"I don't know, Case. It's just I got this cold feeling in here," he tapped his chest with a gloved fist, "that these tracks might belong to the fellers that have been following us."

"But why would they suddenly get ahead us?"

Brazos shrugged. "If it is them it could be they've guessed where we're headed…or maybe they aim to bushwhack us."

"Oh. How many are there?" she asked staring at the tracks.

"Well, I count six horses. 'Course one or two might be pack animals."

Brazos paced several steps and then back. He looked up at Casey Sue. She threw him a questioning look.

"What are you thinking?" she queried.

"Well, if it is them—an' I'm not saying it is, but just in case—I reckon we ought to pull an Indian trick on them. We'll track them instead of the other way around."

CHAPTER ELEVEN

They had come upon the cabin abruptly and quickly jerked their horses back out of sight from where they surveyed the small log structure and surroundings. The cabin must have been one long abandoned that these men had stumbled upon and intended to use for the night. For the past two hours Brazos and Casey Sue had been following the tracks of the six horses. The small corral in back of the cabin contained six horses. One was the big bay.

"Case, I reckon they're hold up here for the night," Brazos said grimly.

"What are we going to do?" she asked never taking her eyes from the cabin.

"Well, I reckon we wait 'til dark. Then I'll slip down there and a have a look-see. Those six horses worry me. I'm not shore how many hombres are hold-up in there. 'Couse them riders might not even be the ones we're looking for."

"I'm going with you—"

"Like hell you are!" Brazos cursed.

"An' just what do you expect me to do while you go gallivanting around?" she demanded.

Hard gray eyes clashed with hers. "I reckon you'll stay here where it's safe."

"Brazos Kincaid, I happen to have an interest in what comes about—or have you forgotten?"

"Shore, I reckon you're right, but you're my responsibility and I ain't about to let anything happen to you! You stay here! I mean it," he said glaring at her.

Casey Sue glowered back at the man. His harsh words had not taken her by surprise. Ever since that incident at the hotel he had been like an overly protective parent. It was getting on her nerves, but she decided not to argue, for now. She stared at him in cool silence her temper rising. She was not about to listen to a word he said. She would simply bide her time. She didn't speak to him again waiting for night to fall.

"Mind me now. Stay here," he admonished once more before taking off his spurs and slipping silently into the darkness.

Casey Sue figured it was well after midnight as she settled to wait. It seemed like an hour had passed, but it probably hadn't been that long. But he should have been back by now, unless something happened to him. She had no doubt now that it was her uncle's murderers in the cabin, and—God what if they caught Brazos, or even—no, she wouldn't think that. Several more minutes passed. She could stand it no longer. Getting to her feet she clutched her Winchester in a tight grip and set off the way Brazos had gone. There was no moon and the night was black. By bending low she was able to make out the dark silhouette of the cabin's roof against the lighter gray sky. The wind brought a whiff of wood smoke. Her heart pounded as she stealthily circled the cabin. The yellow glow of lantern light marked the single window. She approached slowly, cautiously. What had happened to Brazos? Minutes later Casey Sue heard voices. She hunkered down holding her breath as she slipped beneath the window. A woman's wild laugh suddenly made her blood freeze.

"You're a bungling oaf, cowboy." There was the sound of a blow, something hard striking flesh. "Now, I'm going to ask you again, an' if you know what's good for you, you had better answer. Where's the girl?"

That voice. She had heard it before. Holding her breath Casey Sue warily peeked over the window sill. Her heart felt as if it would burst when she saw her uncle's former companion, Flo Morgan standing over Brazos who was tied to a chair, hands behind his back. It took all of Casey Sue's self-control not to rush inside. She sunk down heart pounding. 'Think, Casey Sue,' she chided herself. Flo Morgan. What was she doing here; she was supposed to be in San Antonio! An icy chill swept over her.

"Damn it to hell," she breathed, Flo Morgan had a hand in her uncle's death, his murder! She had not gone, as she said, to San Antonio, but…she let out another muffled curse—and she had *liked* the woman. Slowly she lifted her head and took another peek through the window. She couldn't seem to stop shivering. Flo Morgan still hovered over Brazos. There was blood on his lips. Besides Brazos and the woman two others occupied the small single room cabin. All were slovenly.

Leaning a bony shoulder against the ladder extending upward to a makeshift loft to Casey Sue's left, with a long expressionless face, thin and sharp, was the skeletal-thin man she had seen on the stairs the day her uncle was murdered. Standing next to Flo was a big heavy-shouldered man. His dark bearded face showed lines left by wildness, dissipation. There were shadows under black eyes in a reckless, careless, sinister visage. She knew without a doubt this was the man who had forced his way into her hotel room in El Paso and beat her. She slumped back down gripping her Winchester tightly. There came the sickening crunch of bone on flesh. Oh, they were beating Brazos! She had to do something, they were beating him. Creeping around the corner of the cabin she halted in front of the door. Slowly but deftly she cocked her rifle. She stood and noiselessly pushed open the door, took a step inside.

"Hands up!" she shouted.

Startled faces turned toward her. A sneer curved the big man lips. Skeletal man straightened his bulging eyes taking her in.

"One of you hombres cut my pard's hands free," she ordered, rifle trained on the hulking man facing her.

Suddenly an arm snaked around her waist from behind and a hand grasped her Winchester. The rifle discharged with a loud crack drowning her cry of impotent outrage as the weapon was snatched from her grip. Someone struck her hard in her back and she was sent sprawling. That same somebody knelt upon her back and her arms were jerked behind her and her wrists bound tightly. She lay for a moment numb in body and mind. Fool. Why hadn't she stopped to think they would have a lookout posted?

"How bad is he hit?" Flo Morgan's voice reached her ears. She sounded furious.

'Who was she talking about?' Casey Sue wondered. Had her bullet struck someone? 'Oh, God, not Brazos!'

"I reckon it's bad," said another voice. "Plumb through the gut."

Casey Sue swallowed the bile rising in her throat.

"Buck," spoke up that same voice, "I reckon yu're bad shot. Yu don't have long."

"Buck?" Casey Sue gasped exhaling a long relieved breath. Not Brazos! Thank God!

There came a shuffling of feet and mumbled curses. Casey Sue closed her eyes, torn between elation that she had shot one of the desperados and horror that she may have taken a man's life. She became aware suddenly of Brazos' whispered voice.

"Case, are you hurt?" he breathed anxiously looking back over his shoulder at her.

She lay on her back peering up at Brazos, hands tied behind him, on the chair a few feet away. Blood trickled from the corner of his mouth and one eye looked puffy.

"I'm fine, only mad at myself," she sniffled. "I forgot about them having a lookout."

"Damn it, Case. I told you to stay put," he hissed.

"I'm sorry," she sobbed.

"Don't cry," he pleaded. "I'll think of something."

She sucked in her breath as Flo Morgan's figure hovered over her. For a long moment she stared down at Casey Sue then she ripped open her coat and jerked the packet containing the claim form and the map free.

"Nice of you to come barging in," she said, "Saved me lots of trouble. You were beginning to irritate me."

"Why?" Casey Sue breathed.

"Why?" Flo repeated a wicked smile curving her lips. "Why, child, I needed this," she sneered opening the packet and glancing eagerly at the contents. "And I wanted you out of the way. Your silly uncle put your name on that claim form, so you had to be taken care of. I don't want any loose ends."

"Uncle Will—you—"

She laughed. "Of course, you stupid girl. He was a silly fool. Now I have all I need, the claim form—and the map as well." She turned her back upon Casey Sue then and went to where the big man she'd call Buck lay propped against the wall.

"It won't be long now," the man kneeling beside Buck said. The man who was talking, he must have been the one who grabbed her from behind Casey Sue thought.

Flo bent over the wounded man. "Buck, do you want anything, water, whiskey?"

Buck's eyelids fluttered open. He looked up at her with eyes gradually losing their light. They blinked, once then slowly closed. He made no response.

"Is he gone?" Flo asked.

"I reckon he's still hanging on," the man beside Buck said. He was a spare, gaunt man with a face strikingly white beside the darkly hued man propped against the wall. A thick black mustache hung down past his mouth and a heavy lock of greasy black hair hung down over one eye.

"Hmm," Flo murmured brow furrowing.

"What yu figurin'?"

"We leave in the morning," she said circumspectly.

"What about Buck?"

"We leave at first light no matter. I want as many miles between me and this cabin before dark," Flo replied evasively. It was obvious who was giving the orders.

Pete's deep-set hollow eyes met Casey Sue's. "What about the girl?" he growled.

"I don't have time for your foolishness. You can have as many of them Mexican hussies you want when we get to Pinos Altos," the woman growled. "Now get some sleep, both of you, we got a long ride tomorrow."

Pete grunted but said no more. Flo stretched out on the narrow bunk. "Pete, you and Rattlesnake take turns watching," she ordered. "An' leave the girl alone, you hear!"

Propped against the wall, arms bound behind her back Casey Sue kept a watchful eye on the three desperados, especially the one Flo called Pete, but thankfully he did not approach her as the night waned. Casey Sue's head suddenly jerked upright. She glanced quickly around heart beating rapidly. All was quiet. She must have dosed off. She had been determined to remain awake. Her shoulders ached from having her arms tied behind her. Brazos sat unmoving, head bent to his chest. Asleep she imagined. She debated trying calling to him, but decided against it. She didn't want to rouse the others. She wiggled her fingers attempting to maintain some feeling in them.

Voices startled her. She must have dozed off again. Through the lone window she could see the gray light of approaching dawn. Somebody lit a lamp and she blinked her eyes against the sudden brightness.

"Case, are you all right?" Brazos whispered.

"Yes, just stiff and cramped," she whispered back, relieved to hear his voice.

"How is he?" Flo said coming to peer down at the still form of the big man.

"Daid," Pete replied flatly. "Sumtime during the night. Never made a sound."

"Rattlesnake, rustle up some breakfast, and then see to the pack horses," Flo ordered.

Casey Sue's stomach growled as the aroma of sourdough biscuits and beans filled her nostrils. She closed her eyes at the sound of clinking spoons on metal plates as they ate. Shortly picking up a pack under each arm Pete and the skinny one called Rattlesnake stalked out of the cabin. Flo followed. Casey Sue stared as the door slammed closed behind her. They were leaving them here? She shook her head disbelievingly. A minute later Pete pushed open the door and entered. He carried a lariat rope. He looped the rope around Brazos' ankles tying him snuggly to the chair after which he secured the chair to the ladder leading up to the loft. The man turned then to Casey Sue. He grinned wolfishly and bent over her, eyes piercing. He reached a hand fumbling to unbuckle the belt at her waist.

"Get your filthy hands off me!" she screamed.

The cabin door opened. "Pete," Flo snarled. "What the hell are you doing? Tie the girl's ankles and let's get moving."

Pete growled under his breath. Under Flo's watchful eye he proceeded to tie her ankles together tightly before getting to his feet. He stared hungrily down at her for a long moment.

"What a waste," he muttered and stormed out of the cabin.

Casey Sue sucked in a shuddering breath. Did they leave them here to starve?

"Damn that feller shore knows how to tie a knot," Brazos cursed. "I can't move my hands or my feet. How about you, Case?"

She shook her head, before realizing he couldn't see her from where he sat. "I can't feel my hands," she said as a tear slid down one cheek.

Suddenly she jerked her head up as a strong whiff of burning wood filled her nostrils. It took a moment before realization dawned.

"Brazos!" she cried. "Oh my God, they're set the cabin on fire!"

Brazos could smell it now; the pungent smell of burning wood. He darted a look upward and saw dark gray smoke curling around the underside of the cedar roof shingles. Be damn! They had set the cabin on fire! They intended to burn them alive! His heart began to pound loudly in his chest as he struggled against the ropes that bound his wrists. There was no give in them. He twisted his head back over his shoulder trying to see Casey Sue. From his position he could see her legs from the knees down. A rope trussed them tightly together.

"Case, can you stand?"

He could hear her frightened panting breath as she squirmed and thrashed about.

"It's no use, Brazos," she sobbed digging her spurs into the dirt floor.

The smoke on the underside of the roof shingles was thicker and darker, spreading outward toward the log walls and the hissing crackle of flames was louder.

"Case can you scoot closer; and raise your feet so I can reach your spurs. Maybe I can use them to slice through these ropes."

She didn't answer but he could hear her twisting and wiggling. Soon her booted soles thudded against the back of his chair.

"Good girl!" he said as he fumbled to find the rowels of her Mexican spurs with his bound wrists. After a long moment of groping he gave a frustrated curse. "Whenever I try to saw through the rope, the rowels keep spinning. It's not gonna work."

Another long moment passed with only the sound of Casey Sue's soft weeping.

"Case, I have an idea. Can you turn onto your stomach? I think then if you raise your feet and brace your spurs against the chair back the rowels won't move. That may just do the trick."

Grunting and cursing under her breath, Casey Sue managed to turn herself over on her stomach, and with more cursing she bobbed up and down like an inch worm using her chin and knees to catapult herself along until she could place her booted feet against the back of the chair. Smoke began to cloud the room and she held her breath feeling her legs jiggling and vibrating as Brazos worked his hands back and forth sawing through the rope with the sharp rowels of her spurs. It seemed an eternity before he cried out in triumph as his wrists sprang free.

"Thank God!" she sobbed.

He rubbed his wrists and hands together vigorously bringing feeling back, then fumbling in his pocket for his jackknife he quickly sliced through the ropes about his ankles. Standing, he stomped his feet as blood rushed back into his legs before kneeling and cutting Casey Sue free. He helped her to her feet and with a cry she flung her arms about his neck. He clasped her tightly against his chest for several heartbeats then pushed her away.

"Come on, Case, let's get the hell out of here."

Coughing, taking shallow breaths, the thickening smoke stinging her eyes, she nodded. With one hand covering his nose and mouth, Brazos ducked beneath the gathering haze of sooty smoke and quickly surveyed the room. Casey Sue's Winchester lay in the corner where it had been tossed, his own Colt and hers a few feet away. He holstered his and thrust her rifle and Colt into her hands. Flame burst through the shingles overhead as he grabbed her wrist and dragged her to the door and out into the early morning light where they each hauled in great gasps of the cool air.

CHAPTER TWELVE

By the time they reached the place where they had left their horses the mental numbness at having escaped being burned alive had faded, and Brazos suddenly let go a string of curses. Casey Sue added her own as she collapsed on the grass as though drained of strength. Then she began to laugh. She knew very well, recognized the fact she was on the brink of hysteria, but she couldn't stop laughing. Brazos broke off his curses and stared down at her as though she had grown two heads. A moment later he dropped down beside her and tossing an arm over her shoulder joined her.

She stopped laughing as quickly as she had began, and turned and threw her arms about his waist and buried her face in the curve of his shoulder knocking the sombrero from her head.

"I wore—my spurs."

"I'm shore glad you did—"

"But I—I almost didn't! I planned to take them off, like you did. Only I—forgot—in my excitement. What would have happened if—if I had not?"

"Hush," he murmured wrapping his arms about her hesitantly. "Don't think about it."

She was silent for a long moment and he could feel the flutter of her distraught breath against his neck. Her body suddenly grew taut.

"Damn it all to hell!" she cursed. "They stole the papers from me!"

"Ah-huh," he grunted.

She pulled back from him eyes searching his. "You look terrible. Your upper lip is split open. At least it's stopped bleeding."

"Yeah, I reckon that hombre can shore punch," he grunted.

"Hold still and I'll clean off the blood," she said and going to her saddle she brought back a canteen. He closed his eyes enjoying the feel of her fingers as she gently washed his face.

"There's a knot the size of your fist on your left cheek, and I reckon you'll have a huge black eye by tomorrow morning," she grinned.

"It's not funny," he grumbled.

"I'm sorry," she apologized unconvincingly getting to her feet. "What are we going to do now?"

"Well, I reckon I shore got a bone to pick with that lady—"

"She's no lady," Casey Sue spat.

He gave a humorless chuckle. "No, I reckon she ain't. That woman is bad medicine."

"We're going after them, right?" she said with finality.

"Yeah, we shore are," he said as they both peered down the incline at the cabin now fully engulfed in flame. "We best eat a bite, and then get started."

"Brazos, without the map, do you think you could find the way there?" she asked anxiously.

"Shore. I reckon when I close my eyes I can still see that map plain as ever," he answered conficently. "But I reckon that only gets us to the end point on your uncle's map. Whatever he meant by that other stuff we'll find out when we get there."

Midmorning the following day they halted. It was a big country, exceedingly wild and rough. They climbed a ridge and kept to its summit for most of the morning. If Brazos' memory of Uncle Wills' map was accurate they were not far from his claim. Tomorrow would find them finally at their destination.

"Case, I reckon we're awful close to your uncles' claim," Brazos said peering out across the valley below. "Didn't you say your Uncle Will had a partner?"

Casey Sue nodded. "His name is Joshua Gaines according to the papers Uncle Will gave me."

"Well, it's been more'n two months since your uncle left to find you. I hope your uncle's pard is all right."

From his vantage point on the high slope Brazos peered out across the valley below. Suddenly his eye caught sight of what appeared to be a cabin set against the opposite hillside sheltered by tall pines.

"Case, I reckon that there cabin must be your uncle's place."

"Oh, Brazos, I don't think I want to go into another cabin, ever. Not after our last experience," she shuttered. "My clothes still stink of smoke."

"Shore I reckon," Brazos retorted. "But it shore fits the details of the map as I recollect."

Brazos studied the crudely built cabin but could see no activity about the place. His gaze moved to the rough cedar pole corral a short distance from the cabin. The gate to the corral stood open. At the edge of a grassy area west of the cabin he spied a burro. It was dragging its lead rope as it leisurely grazed.

"That's queer," Brazos muttered studying the silent and lifeless cabin.

"What is it?" Casey Sue asked anxiously. She suddenly found herself extremely nervous. Where were Flo and her two murdering sidekicks?

They had her uncle's map, so they must have discovered this cabin. Had they murdered Mr. Gaines? Well, for one thing Flo wouldn't be expecting her and Brazos to be on her trail.

The burro had what appeared to be a single-rig pack hitched to its back and Brazos could plainly see a shovel and pick-ax tied to the pack. No smoke came from the chimney.

"Something don't seem right, Case," he said. "That burro's all packed and ready to go somewhere, but there's no one around that I can see."

"Could, you know, could they have found this place—got here before us?" she asked uneasily. She didn't need to explain who *they* were.

"I reckon it's possible. That's what worries me. But I don't see any sign of life around the cabin except for the burro."

"Maybe it's an ambush," Casey Sue mused grimly.

"Hah!" Brazos flung out. "Who are they going to bushwhack? They reckon for shore we're dead."

"Well, I guess you're right, now that you reminded me," she smiled unreservedly.

The trail led down past the cabin and they started off down the steep grade. When they were within a hundred feet or so of the cabin Brazos called out. There was no answer from within. The burro looked up at them indifferently, then lowered his head and continued grazing. Brazos peered about, listening, and then he slowly dismounted.

"You wait here, Case," he ordered.

Holding the big roan's reins he walked up to the cabin door. He called again loudly, but there came no response. He tried the door and found it unlocked, and slowly pushed it open. He peered into the dim interior. There was no one inside. There were two narrow bunks set in one corner. On the opposite side he saw a small iron cooking stove. A crude wood table set in the center of the room. A few articles of clothing hung from a pole in one corner. Along one wall were three shelves stacked with sundry can goods. A bowl and a tin cup sat on the table next to a kerosene lantern. The place was not untidy and it had an obvious lived-in look.

Brazos retraced his steps walking back outside and stood peering about, undecided as to what to do.

"What are you thinking?" Casey Sue asked worriedly.

"You got me, Case. There's no sign of trouble, like a fight or some disturbance. It's not like someone to go off and leave his animal unattended though," he said shaking his head.

Brazos walked around to the rear of the cabin and saw a workbench against the cabin wall under a rude overhang. It contained several well-used tools. He called out again. The white flags of several deer moved rapidly up the opposite slope, but no human sound was heard. He walked back around to the front of the cabin and peered up at Casey Sue. She was staring down at what appeared to be tracks in the dirt. He walked over to where she was. There were many old booted footprints in the dirt.

He stepped into the saddle and walked the horse out a ways from the cabin surveying the ground for sign. Casey Sue followed. There was a worn path leading up into a deep wild oak and cedar-lined gorge. Boot tracks were plain here as well as those of the burro and a keen study showed the most recent boot tracks going away from the cabin. Overlaying the boot prints in several places were the hoof prints of the burro coming back this way.

"You see what I see, Case?" Brazos said.

"Ah-huh. The only tracks coming back this way are those of the burro. It looks like the burro returned without its owner."

"Yeah, that's what I make out."

The path led up the narrow aisle of grassy assent between wooded slopes.

"I reckon we ought to have a look yonder up this path."

Casey Sue said nothing but started off up the trail following Brazos. Presently he espied the top of an oak shrub leaning over distorted and striking as though violently wrenched, and perhaps as recent as a day or two ago. This drew his sharp attention. In the dirt it was plain to see deep scuffmarks leading off the trail.

"Brazos! Look there!" Casey Sue cried leaping from her horse and pointing down the side of the hill.

Perhaps fifty feet down the oak and jack pine slope Brazos saw what appeared to be the legs and booted feet of a man.

"I reckon that slope's too steep and treacherous for a horse," he said stepping from the saddle and dropping the reins. "Stay here. I'm gonna have a look."

Casey Sue came to the edge of the path peering intently down at the figure as Brazos started working his way cautiously down the slope, digging in with his booted feet. As he slowly made his way Brazos noticed the telltale broken branches and plough marks in the dirt where someone had tumbled and slid down the sheer incline. Reaching the figure he saw an older man perhaps in his sixties. His gray-white hair was cloaked with dust. His shirt and overalls were covered with dirt as well and ripped in several places apparently as a result of his fall down the slope. A cut on the man's forehead had bled profusely, but had since clotted. Brazos gently placed a hand on the man's chest. He opened his eyes peered hazy-eyed up at Brazos.

"Where—did you—come from?" he rasped, weakly.

"Never mind that. How bad are you hurt?" Brazos replied.

"W-water," the man croaked.

"Shore thing, old timer. Lay still."

"Case toss down one of the canteens," Brazos yelled back up the slope to Casey Sue.

Instead of throwing the canteen, she started down the slope much as he had digging her booted feet into the dirt balancing herself with one hand while holding the canteen out in the air with the other. Brazos gave her an angry glare when she reached him, but she ignored him.

"Is he hurt bad?" she asked.

"Don't know," he answered uncorking the canteen and bending gently lifted the man's head a few inches and placed the mouth of the canteen to his parched and cracked lips. He drank greedily. Casey Sue knelt and tenderly took the man's head in her lap.

"Joshua Gaines?" she asked softly.

"Thet's—me. Who air—yu?" he rasped rolling his eyes back in his head trying to see her.

"My name is Casey Sue Thornton. Will Thornton was my uncle," she replied.

"Willie? He's back?" he growled. "Wal, I reckon—it's 'bout—time."

Casey Sue's eyes met Brazos'. She didn't respond.

"How long have you been laid up here?" Brazos asked.

Gaines shook his head weakly. "Don't—know—days—I reckon. Damn jackass—got spooked—knocked me—"

"It's all right, old timer, save your breath. Let's get you up to the trail."

Brazos made his way back up the steep incline to where both horses stood, bridles dragging the ground. Brazos unfastened his lariat and the one from Casey Sue's saddle. Each rope was slightly more than thirty feet in length. He would need both ropes to reach the injured man as it must be at least fifty feet to where he laid head nestled in Casey Sue's lap. After linking the two ropes he fastened the end of one to his saddle horn, and started back down the slope.

The frail-looking old man couldn't have weighed much more than a hundred-twenty pounds. As gentle as he could Brazos hoisted him onto his back.

"Case, go on back up and steer my horse. Make shore he don't haul us up too fast," he instructed.

He waited as she scrambled back up the slant. Then he clasped the old man's arm, which was about his neck with one hand to keep him from slipping. With his other hand he clutched the lariat rope, and started working his way gradually up the incline as Casey Sue slowly backed his horse. The big roan kept the rope stretched taut pulling Brazos with the injured Gaines slung over his back, up the steep ascent. Brazos's shirt was soaked with sweat by the time they reached the path on top of the ridge. As gentle as he could he lifted the old man up into the saddle while Casey Sue coiled the two lariat ropes. All the while Gaines never made a sound, but hunched over the saddle horn breathing deeply. Brazos led the big roan down the path to the cabin. Casey Sue rode ahead and hurried into the cabin where she made one of the bunks ready for Gaines.

"How you doing old timer?" Brazos asked as he laid him on the narrow bunk.

"I'm—shore—obliged te yu—an' yu lass. I reckon—I'd of—cashed in my chips—out thyar if yu hadn't found me."

"My name's Brazos Kincaid. Like Case here said, she's Will Thornton's niece."

"Kincaid, huh. Wal, I'm rite glad te meet the both of yu. Say, where's Willie anyhow?"

"Oh, Mr. Gaines," Casey Sue cried, "Uncle Will is dead—murdered!"

"Murdered, yu say?" he growled, twisting his head his keen gaze seeking Casey Sue's. "Tell me—how?"

"I reckon somebody must have discovered—about the gold strike. They forced their way into his hotel room—stabbed him.

"He must have—let sumthin' slip, 'bout the gold."

"I reckon so, Mr. Gaines," she said sadly. "That's what I figured. They searched him and the room, but they didn't find the claim form cause he'd given it to me for safekeeping."

"Ah," he muttered. "He got the claim—filed."

"Yes, Mr. Gaines. He shore did. He told me about you and him being partners."

He sighed wearily. "I'm sorry lass. Willie was—a good man, shore did his—part. But yu come—saved me. Thet shore—means a bunch te me—an' I'm shore glad he—found yu before—" he sighed patting her hand weakly.

"Me, too, Mr. Gaines. At least I got to be with him for a short while. But—Oh Mr. Gaines, me and Brazos was bushwhacked by the same murdering skunks that killed Uncle Will. They stole the claim form and the map Uncle Will made showing the location of the gold strike. They tied us up in an old abandoned cabin and set it on fire, but we escaped."

The old prospector closed his eyes and let out a deep raspy sigh. "Wal, I reckon they'll try to bushwhack us, too."

"That's what I figure," Brazos said. "What I don't figure is why they haven't. They had a head start on me and Case. Fact is when I saw your body half way down that slope; I thought for shore they had killed you. By the way, how'd you wind up down the side of that mountain, anyhow?"

"That—damn Gus! Where is he, anyhow?" he demanded, trying to lift his head.

"Who's Gus?"

"That ornery—cuss of a—jackass of—mine."

Brazos grinned. "Well, I reckon he's out yonder on that grassy spot west of the cabin eating his fill."

"Ah," Gaines sighed. "Does he—still have his—pack?"

"Yep."

"Kincaid, could yu—turn him inte the corral, an—an tote his pack bag in hyar?"

"Shore. Case will stay here with you."

"Yeah. I'll jest rest a—bit."

The burro was easy to catch and Brazos walked the animal up to the cabin where he untied the pick-ax and shovel that was tied on top of the canvas pack cover. Stacking the pick-ax and shovel against the side of the cabin he removed the canvas pack cover. As he did so a small leather bag fell to the ground. He reached and picked it up and was amazed at how heavy it was. Curious, he loosened the thong and opened the flap and peered inside. It was full of what he realized were shiny gold nuggets.

"I'll be damn," he exclaimed under his breath. "Looks like Uncle Will and the old man shore did strike it rich. I admit I was some doubting it."

He quickly re-tied the flap and stuffed the bag inside the pack bag with the other items, which he saw were cooking utensils. He unfastened the pack bag from the pack tree and sat it on the ground by the front door. He then led the burro over to the corral and put him inside. He undid the lash cinch and slid the well-used single-rig packsaddle and blanket off and tossed it over one of the fence rails. He went out and closed the gate. When he reached the cabin he picked up the pack bag and carried it inside and dropped it at the foot of Gaines' bunk.

"Thanks, Kincaid," Gaines said weakly.

"No thanks needed, Mr. Gaines," Brazos drawled. "I reckon I'll just have a look around."

Clutching his Winchester in one hand, he stepped outside.

"Let me have a look at that cut on your forehead," Casey Sue said and bent to inspect the wound. It was an ugly cut and had bled a lot, but had clotted on its own leaving dried blood crusted on Gaines' forehead and cheek.

"Looks like you bunged your head pretty good," she remarked, "I'll wash off all that dried blood and bandage it up 'fore it starts bleeding again."

Casey Sue poured water from the large water bucket on the small cupboard in one corner into the shallow wash pan she found next to it. Dipping a cup towel into the water, she gently cleaned the blood from Gaines' face and bandaged the wound with one of the old man's bandanas that had seen more than a few washings.

"Mr. Gaines," Casey Sue murmured after she saw that the man was resting comfortably, "Did Uncle Will b-bring a woman up here?"

"A woman yu say? Wal, lass, I never seed him with no woman. Not hyar anyhow," he said. "I reckon the only woman he talked about was yu. He shore loved yu, lass. Talked regularly 'bout goin' back an' findin' yu and yur paw. Said he wanted te make it up te yu—thet now with his share of the gold, the three of yu could go inte ranchin' like yu always planned. I reckon his share belongs te yu now, lass," he said gray eyes boring into hers.

"Oh," she sighed. "I hadn't thought of that."

She was silent for a long moment. "Mr. Gaines, I reckon I ought to tell you. I'm shore worried. Like Brazos said them bushwhackers had a head start, and the map; why haven't they showed up?"

"Shore, that's a worry," he said. Then after a moment, "Why'd yu asked 'bout a woman, lass?"

"She's the leader of the bunch," Casey Sue burst out. "She calls herself Flo Morgan. There were three desperados with her, but I reckon there's only two now."

She went on to tell about finding Brazos tied up in the cabin and getting caught from behind and how her wayward shot wounded one of the desperados.

"He was the one who murdered Uncle Will; him and the one called Rattlesnake—his name shore fits. He's tall and as skinny as a stick and twice as mean. The one I shot died that night. So now there's just Flo and Rattlesnake and the other worm, she called Pete."

"I reckon yu've had a rough time, lass, loosin' yur paw an' then poor Willie murdered; an' then yu was almost kilt."

She nodded solemnly. "Uncle Will told me about you, Mr. Gaines, that you were his partner," she smiled shyly. "Uncle Will spoke highly of you. I'd shore like it if you'll be my friend."

"Wal, shore," Gaines said. "I'd be proud to be yur friend, lass."

"Oh, I felt you would. Somehow you remind me of my paw."

"Wal, lass, that shore is sweet for me te heah. I never had a girl, or boy, either, an' God knows I've missed a lot... Won't yu tell me yur story, lass?"

"Do you feel up to it? It's a long and sad story, Mr. Gaines."

"I reckon I'd like te heah it."

"Well, my mother died when I was fifteen—swamp fever paw said. You see we lived on a plantation in Louisiana. Things never were the same after the war and when mama died paw decided to come west. So, Uncle Will, paw and me—that's all the family I had—we left Louisiana. We had a canvas covered wagon, and eight horses. I rode and drove for months I reckon. Somewhere near San Antonio Uncle Will left us. Paw said we was going too slow to suit him. He said Uncle Will would meet us at the next town. But he never showed up, and then paw—he was bit by a rattlesnake over near Sweetwater. There wasn't no doctor. He—he died two days later.

I was left on my own, so I took to dressing like a boy. I had to earn my living, and being a girl made it hard. And I shore hated to be a servant. Most men treated me fine, but there were some, who—who wanted me. I got a job wrangling horses for a trail driving outfit going up to Kansas City. Lucky for me when the drive was over I got hired on with the boss, Abe Brasee. He had a big ranch just south of San Antonio. I reckon he suspected I was a girl, but he treated me nice, kind of watched out for me. I liked it there, but—I was shore…lonely, having no real folks and all. Then Uncle Will showed up at the ranch. He didn't know about paw's death. He was shore put out feeling that he had let me and paw down, but he swore things would be much better. He said he had this place, a ranch o'er New Mexico he was fixing to buy. We'd have a home of our own—"

"Yep, thet's what yur uncle told me. He was shore lookin' forward te the day," Gaines said wistfully.

"Oh, that makes me sadder than ever," she sighed, eyes moist.

— CHAPTER THIRTEEN —

Casey Sue watched over Gaines, nursed him when his fever raged the first two days. For an old man—she wasn't certain his age, but guessed he must be in his seventies—he had turned out to be a tough old codger. Brazos had no explanation as to why Flo and her bunch had not made an appearance. There was only one way into the small sheltered canyon and Brazos kept a sharp lookout. Casey Sue could tell he was worried. That evening as they ate supper Brazos offhandedly related that he was going to scout back up the trail in the morning. Casey Sue hadn't been fooled by his casual tone and after they finished eating and Brazos walked outside, she followed as far as the door and stood watching him. Brazos sat on the bench to the left of the door and began cleaning his Colt. It gleamed in the evening sunlight slanting through the trees like polished steel. He appeared absorbed in his task. His brow was corded and dark, the line of his cheek tight. Casey Sue sat down beside him on the bench. Brazos glanced at her out of the corner of his eye, but said nothing; nor did she as she peered out at the peaceful, evening pastoral scene. A soft breeze stirred her soft golden curls and waved the grass sloping down to the stream. Birds chirped their evening song. Overhead the sky spread blue darkening to the east.

"I reckon I ought to go with you in the morning," she said not looking at him.

"And why would you want to do that?" he asked turning slightly to look at her.

"Shore, you might need my help," she said.

"Ah, Case," Brazos expostulated seemingly offended. "Shore I owe you my life on more'n one occasion, but I reckon I can handle this."

Casey Sue stared at Brazos uncertain how to respond and watched silently as he stood and walked off toward the corral. Finally she got to her feet and went back into the cabin where she gathered up the dirty dishes and began to wash them and stack them in the cabinet. Brazos hadn't returned by the time she said goodnight to Mr. Gaines and retired behind the tarpaulin that separated her living space from the rest of the cabin. She undressed and slid under the blankets staring up at the rough shingles above her feeling disheartened and without the slightest idea why. When she woke the next morning she hurriedly dressed and pulled aside her makeshift curtain. Her gaze went quickly to the spot against the wall where Brazos normally unrolled his bedroll. The bedroll was there neatly folded. Mr. Gaines stirred and slowly sat up scratching one white-bearded cheek.

"I reckon your friend left 'bout half hour ago. Said not te wake yu, thet he'd be back 'fore dark," the old man said.

Casey Sue said nothing and went about fixing breakfast.

Brazos spotted buzzards circling high in the sky to the west as he slowly descended the narrow trail. He watched their wide gliding path round and round, his curiosity growing as their numbers increased. Something big, he decided, an animal, but then there was the constant danger of marauding bands of Mescalero Apaches. It was possible some way station or ranch could have fallen victim to their violence. He extracted his Winchester from his saddle boot and held it across his lap as he continued along the rough seldom-used trail.

Brazos began to feel the strain of suspense the closer he drew to the spot where the buzzards circled. At length, about midmorning he halted at the head of a shallow ravine from where a stream trickled. A breeze issuing from the rocky gorge brought with it the smell of something foul. He studied the ground. The imprint of horse hoofs was easily visible in the sandy ground. He studied them closely looking for unshod hoofs that would indicate Indians, but those he saw were all shod with steel shoes. They appeared maybe a day or two old.

On slow steps his horse advanced into the low-walled ravine. The scent of death grew stronger along with his apprehension. He heard the keen nicker of a horse before he came fully upon the scene. He stared. The canyon widened and beneath the shade of several scrub oak lay three bodies. A picket rope stretched between two other oaks where five horses were tied. They strained at their halter ropes doubtlessly frantic for water. Two buzzards hopped along the ground before taking to the air, their great black wings spread wide. Brazos pulled his bandana up over his nose as he nudged his horse closer. Two of the bodies lay near to the burned-out campfire; the third some distance away.

Brazos' eyes swept the bodies, and he uttered a grunt when he recognized the body closest to him…Flo Morgan! And it was at that moment she stirred as though sensing his presence. He stepped from the saddle and knelt by her side tugging the bandana away from his nose. Her right hand clutched a Colt pistol, her other hand lay over her stomach. It, as well as her shirt, was soaked in blood. Her eyes fluttered open and she stared up at him for a long moment.

"You!" she finally gasped, her voice barely a whisper. She made as though to lift the Colt, but she hadn't the strength and her hand fell back.

"Is…he dead," she wheezed.

"Who? They're both cashed," he answered.

A crooked smile twisted her lips.

"What happened?" Brazos asked.

"Go to…hell…cowboy," she whispered harshly, and he watched as the light slowly faded from her eyes.

"Well, I shore reckon that's where you're headed, lady," he said grimly.

Brazos leaned back on his haunches scrutinizing the area with a keen eye. The desperado he remembered Flo calling Pete lay on his stomach. Near one hand was a Bowie knife. Its long blade coated with dried blood. There appeared to be three bullet holes in his back. Several paces away flung out on his back lay the skeletal thin outlaw called Rattlesnake. It appeared he had been shot at least twice. His pistol was half way out of its holster. He must have been caught by surprise, or he wasn't very handy with the Colt. Brazos guessed the former. He looked back at Pete. On the ground by his right shoulder was an oilskin packet. Brazos recognized it immediately—Casey Sue's claim papers wrapped in their protective sachet.

What happened here began to take shape. In his mind's eye Brazos could see it transpire with terrible certainty. Flo Morgan lay on her bedroll her boots removed, her gun belt hanging over the saddle horn near her head. She was very possibly asleep when Pete stabbed her several times with his knife. Rattlesnake, who must not have been in on Pete's scheme, was gunned down before he had time to draw. Flo had strength enough to retrieve her Colt and managed to shoot Pete as he moved away, the oilskin packet, which he had snatched from Flo's person, or from her pack, in hand.

"No love lost among thieves," Brazos soliloquized as he retrieved the packet of claim papers and stuffed it into his shirt pocket.

He walked to where the horses were tethered and one by one removed their halters. They immediately made for the shallow stream to drink. He found a shovel and pickaxe in one of the packs and set about digging three graves next to where the bodies rested. He didn't search the corpses, but rolled each of them into the shallow graves he had dug, bedroll and all. He had no desire to procure anything from them. All their gear he tossed into the graves with them. The packs and horse tack he left where it lay.

It was twilight when he finally finished and he sat on one of the packs, drained. He wiped his sweaty face with his bandana and stared up at the darkening sky. Night would be on him before he made it back to the old prospector's cabin. He'd have to spend the night in the open; but not here in this canyon; death's hand still lingered here. He hadn't brought his bedroll; intending to be back before dark. It would be a rough night with only his slicker for a bed, but he didn't want to venture traveling at night in this strange country. And he wanted to get away from this canyon and its gruesome secret.

As Brazos worked he had time to think. No threat remained now; Flo Morgan's gang was no more, victims of their own greed, which meant that Casey Sue could claim her share of the gold without fear. So much had happened since that day she had saved his worthless hide. He had to admit when he insisted he and Case were partners he was sincere. But he had been more than a little skeptical about there being a gold mine. He hadn't known then that Case was actually a girl. And things suddenly changed when he made that discovery. His life had never been the same from that day forward. But she was a rich woman now. Where did that leave him? He owned nothing but his horse and tack…and the Colt on his hip. A man had his pride. A man protected his woman, provided for her, not the other way around.

Casey Sue walked to the head of the trail and stood for a long time watching, hoping, for any sight of Brazos. She returned silent and fretful pacing back and forth between the corral and the cabin. What if something happened to Brazos? What if he never returned? She chided herself. He had left his bedroll; he had no intention of staying the night on the trail. Of course he would return—unless… She couldn't stop her pacing. Flo Morgan and her henchmen were still out there. If Brazos met up with them he would be all alone. He needed her.

Finally the smell of cooking meat penetrated her thoughts and she realized it was afternoon. She hurried into the cabin to find her uncle's partner busy at the small cook stove.

"I'm sorry Mr. Gaines," she fretted, "I—I just been most out of my head worrying about Brazos."

"Shore, I know thet, lass, but yu got te eat," he declared in lively humor. "Thet hawkeyed Brazos? Wal, I reckon he can take care of himself."

"You think so, Mr. Gaines?" she said with surprising flippancy as she went about setting the table.

As twilight deepened Casey Sue went out and sat on the bench. She stayed there until night closed and the moon came up and silvered the cabin and the small clearing lending a strange serenity to the hour. From somewhere in the distance pealed forth the long, desolate moan of a wolf. Stars paled before the light of the full moon. Slowly, sometime later, she stood and after a wistful look back along the trail, went in to bed. She kept her Colt close.

She slept fitfully, waking at every little sound. Morning didn't come too soon. At the first gray light of dawn filled her small window she was up and dressed. She took up her Winchester from where it stood in one corner and walked outside on quiet steps careful not to wake Mr. Gaines. The sun had not yet risen. A cloudless sky and balmy air attested to promising weather.

Brazos slept in his clothes minus his gun belt using his saddle as a pillow. He fell asleep quickly only to come awake some hours later. The three belted stars he knew were sloping to the west, so the hour was late. The incessant chirping of insects had thinned. The small fire he had lit had burned down low. Coyotes wailed shrilly off to the north. He lay there as all sorts of thoughts came and went in his mind.

He remembered the night in El Paso when Casey Sue was attacked in her room. It was then that he discovered she was a woman, finding her huddled on the floor in that faded threadbare nightgown that did little to hide her femininity. She had looked so vulnerable, her eye swollen and turning black and blue; a pretty and pathetic little figure. He swore to himself that he would protect her with his life. His previously happy-go-lucky existence had come to an end that night.

"Dog-gone," he breathed into the darkness. "I shore am a lost soul."

He lay there and watched the stars pale and die, the east kindle, the gray steal away as if by magic, and his big roan grazing a short distance away take shape. Brazos was hungry. The night before he had eaten a couple of biscuits and downed a can of peaches he had stuffed in his saddlebags. He cursed under his breath; regretful he hadn't packed more, thinking he was only going to be gone a few hours. He wouldn't make that mistake again. What had gotten into him? Well, he knew the answer to that; a golden haired, freckled-face little beauty.

The sun peeped up red over the purple horizon, and all the land took on a rosy sheen. Birds set up a noisy chirping. Brazos paused to take in the fresh radiance of the dawn. Suddenly a lightness came over him bringing a soft smile to his lips. It was time to get underway. He wanted to see the look on Casey Sue's face when he told her about the demise of Flo Morgan and her gang. Aw hell! He just wanted to see her.

CHAPTER FOURTEEN

Casey Sue watched the sun top the line of trees. She felt utterly lost. Where was Brazos? She refused to think of what she would do if he never returned. They had been through so much together she sniffed, remembering the day she had hid in the willow brake and first laid eyes on him. That Goodman fellow would have lynched him had she not intervened. At first she had merely been embarrassed by all Brazos' bragging about his love life. But at some point, she wasn't sure when, she wanted to punch him; angry with the big conceited giraffe for not seeing her for the girl she was, and at the same time dreading what he would do when he did find out. And now? She swallowed hard.

Movement at the head of the trail drew her attention and she quickly got to her feet. She shaded her eyes with one hand, staring. A lone rider on a tall strawberry roan approached. Heart stilling, she searched the lithe rider's wide-shouldered frame for any evidence of a wound. Seeing her, he lifted a hand and waved. She choked back a sob as relief flooded her, and whirling, hurried into the cabin. Sitting on her bunk she blew out a long, slow breath the release of hours of tension leaving her weak.

Brazos rode past the cabin to the corral where he unsaddled his horse and tossed the saddle and blanket over the fence rail. He led the roan into the corral and slipped the bridle, hanging it over the saddle horn. He poured oats in the trough and then went to the stream for water.

Only after seeing to his horse did he return to the cabin. On the ride back from that dark scene in that lonely canyon, he had gone over in his mind what he would tell Casey Sue, savoring the look of joy on her face when he handed her the oilskin packet containing the claim form, and she realized the threat from Flo and her gang was no more.

At the door of the cabin he hesitated fingering the oilskin packet. He took a deep breath and pushed open the door. Casey Sue sat on her bunk, the curtain pulled aside. Her head was bent, but at the sound of the door opening she looked up.

"You're back," she said and he was struck by the unusual tautness in her voice.

He grinned at her and without a glance at Gaines crossed to her and without a word tossed the oilskin packet in her lap.

"W—what?" she started, her dark gaze widening. "Brazos! How—"

He sat on the bunk beside her. "Well, I reckon the news couldn't be no better," he said, and proceeded to tell her the story of finding Flo and her gang dead, victims of insatiable greed. She stared in wide-eyed horror as he related the tale. When he finished she laid her head on Brazos' shoulder and began to weep.

"Case, pard, what are you crying for now? Flo and her gang are done for. They'll not threaten' you anymore," he said softly, "it's all over."

"Oh, Brazos, If—if only dad and Uncle Will know!"

Gaines led Brazos and Casey Sue a quarter mile up the narrow winding trail overlooking the gorge high above the rapidly flowing stream, to where they came upon a bold outcropping that immediately reminded Brazos of a mule's nose. He exchanged a look with Casey Sue and it was clear she recognized it too. It appeared the trail ended there at the unusually shaped rock and Brazos saw nothing that looked like a mine opening. But Brazos soon learned that was an optical illusion.

It wasn't until he was only a few feet away did a narrow path become visible leading past the outcropping and exposed a ridge of white quartz rock laced with yellow.

Casey Sue had never seen raw gold other than the few nuggets her uncle had shown her, she was totally amazed at first seeing the gold ore. For the next two weeks the three of them had worked digging out the gold. Both Brazos and Gaines tried to discourage Casey Sue insisting that the work was too hard, but she refused to listen, and so they gave in.

It was grueling work. Not having the means or equipment to build a stamp mill or mercury to separate the pyrite, they had to resort to digging with pickax and shovel, washing out the gold with water, a long and tedious process, but a rewarding one, nonetheless. Casey Sue, however, turned out to be less hardy and enduring than she had avowed. Still for a slip of a girl she won praise from both men, though they continued to contend that she could do her part just as well by keeping house and seeing to the cooking. After that first week she finally capitulated and a practical and suitable routine was established. When the tired and hungry miners returned each evening it was to find that a spotlessly clean cabin and a hot mouthwatering meal awaited them.

Early two mornings later Casey Sue walked to the edge of the clearing where she stood watching Brazos and Gaines, leading Gus, until they disappeared around a bend in the narrow mountain trail on their way to the claim. Then she stood gazing about. How cold, sweet, intoxicating the air! She guessed it must be early August, but at this altitude frost glistened like diamonds on the long grass. She turned and walked back into the cabin and began cleaning up the breakfast dishes.

After putting away the dishes she sorted through the supplies noting that they were running low on a number of items. She sat at the table and set about making a list, humming softly as she worked. Every now and then she glanced about the cabin. She had grown to love this place despite the cramped accommodations. It had been glorious seeing Brazos every morning when she woke. It had become like keeping house—she felt her cheeks redden. She shouldn't be thinking such thoughts. One day Brazos would ride away and then where would she be?

She shook herself out of her wayward thoughts and focused on her list. She wasn't sure where the nearest town was they could buy supplies as she and Brazos had avoided populated areas on their way here, but she was certain Uncle Josh would know.

In the past three weeks Casey Sue had taken to calling Gaines Uncle Josh. It was an easy thing to do; he reminded her so much of her paw. She couldn't bring herself to call him paw, though. It just didn't seem right, so she had settled on Uncle Josh.

As it grew toward evening she sat on the bench outside the cabin as she had each night waiting for Brazos and Uncle Josh to return. She watched the gold fade from the tips of the spruces and the sky turn gray bringing a cold breeze from higher up. Twilight had enveloped the little clearing nearly in obscurity before she saw them and breathed a sigh of relief. By the time they reached the cabin all was black except the space of sky overhead where pale stars blinked, and grew clear and white, and cold.

"Brazos, you Uncle Josh stayed so late, I was beginning to worry," Casey Sue said.

"Sorry to worry you, Case, but Josh insists it going to rain tomorrow, so we decided to work until we couldn't see anymore," Brazos said flopping on the bench beside her.

Casey Sue woke in the gray of predawn to the sound of rain on the cabin roof. She pulled her blanket tighter about her not wanting to leave the comfortable bed. She sighed after a moment, however, and slipped from beneath the blankets and quickly dressed. Pulling aside one corner of the tarpaulin that separated her living space from the rest of the cabin she peeked out. The other two occupants were still abed. Tip-toeing to the wash basin she splashed water on her face washing the sleep from her eyes then set about building up the fire in the little stove. Filling the coffee pot she placed it on the stove top to boil while she began mixing dough for biscuits.

"Nothing like the smell of brewing coffee the first thing in the morning," Brazos said yawning as he swung his feet to the floor.

Casey Sue glanced over at him and smiled watching him pull on his boots. Gaines sat up scratching one white-bearded cheek.

"Mornin' lass," he said.

"Morning, Uncle Josh," she grinned, which brought a pleased smile to the old man's face.

It rained all that day, which forced them to remain inside. All in all Brazos needed the time to rest, as he was tasked with most of the heavy work of ferreting out the gold nuggets.

"I reckon *Pinos Altos* is the closest place to get supplies," Gaines said that evening. "It's a little town about twenty mile southeast. Just about a day's ride, I reckon."

"Well, when the weather clears, I reckon you and me ought to ride in there, Case," Brazos said.

It rained for the next four days.

CHAPTER FIFTEEN

As far as Brazos was concerned *Pinos Altos* or any other town would have been good to visit and replenish their supplies, but this mining town, almost as rowdy as it had been in its heyday a few years ago, he imagined, was no place for Casey Sue. Brazos had never seen the like. There was a main street upon which to ride or drive or walk at all hours of the day and far into the night, but to do so was a most arduous undertaking, and not at all to Casey Sue's liking.

The Grand Hotel, where Brazos engaged two rooms on the second floor, hummed with activity. Milling about the crowded street were cattlemen, cowhands, buffalo hunters, desperadoes, men in the rough garb of miners and others in dark suits and greasy slick-backed hair that was the mark of the professional gambler or shifty-eyed entrepreneur bent on separating people from their hard-earned money.

Brazos regretted that he hadn't suggested that Casey Sue wear her boy's disguise. Before they went to eat or shop for supplies, he would have her do so. Without her heavy oversized old coat and attired in a soft flannel shirt that flowed easily with her graceful movements, there was no hiding her femininity.

The sun was still up as they left the livery stables where Brazos left the horses. Casey Sue retrieved her old coat and her floppy hat and pulled it low covering her golden curls. They found a restaurant. It was run by a Chinaman and was small but clean and crowded with customers, which, Brazos declared, was a good sign. His quick eye surveyed the customers, all were men and he noted that only a few appeared to be cowboys. The others had the look of miners. They found a table near the window and ordered steak and eggs, and shortly savory food was set before them.

Leaving the restaurant their hunger satisfied Brazos guided Casey Sue through the crowded street elbowing his way in some cases. Casey Sue stuck close to his side, looking much like a wide-eyed youth. It wasn't that Casey Sue had never experienced anything like this wide open town before. Kansas City on her first trail drive had been much like this, only filled with cowboys just off a long trail drive. But her boss, Abe Brasee had taken care of her, watched over her and she had been safe. She glanced up at Brazos' stern face. He would take care of her.

Brazos assessed every passerby that he encountered; miners in worn coats and scruffy boots, black-frocked, shifty-eyed gamblers, teamsters, ragged tramps and even a few cowboys that made up the passing throng.

Midway up the block Casey Sue spotted a sign reading; *MacIntosh, Groceries and Mercantile. Lewis MacIntosh Proprietor.*

"Brazos, look there," she shouted to be heard over the boisterous crowd.

"I see it, Case," he shouted back. "Come on."

Brazos looked around the large store crowded with merchandise— everything from mining equipment, furniture, clothing, hardware, groceries, saddles and harness and farm implements. There were other customers milling about fingering merchandize in the large spread-out store. The outside noise had diminished noticeably once inside the store.

"You got that list of the things we need?" Brazos asked.

She nodded and started down one aisle. Brazos stood back watching. She moved swiftly and efficiently and soon had the store's counter nearly filled with sundry of foodstuffs. From where he waited Brazos kept a watch on customers entering the store. He felt uneasy for some reason he couldn't identify. Casey Sue stood before the counter peering at the items as she mentally reviewed the list.

"Oh, I forgot. Sugar. I'll be right back," she exclaimed to the clerk and turned quickly only to collide with a tall figure approaching the counter.

"Watch where yer goin', boy," the man growled hands clasping her shoulders in a hard grip ready to toss her to the side.

Casey Sue looked up into his angry face and froze unable to breathe.

"What're yu starin' at, boy!" he snarled and then his eyes widened. "Hey, Platt, look what I got here. It's thet kid that was with thet Brazos Kincaid feller."

"Take your paws off my pard, Lovelace," Brazos said, voice crisp and sharp as he took a slow purposeful step forward.

"Shore," Chess Lovelace said shoving her aside his hand hovering over his holstered Colt.

"Case get behind that counter," Brazos said softly, eyes never turning a breath of a hair from the man he was facing even though he was aware of the dark figure stepping to the side of Lovelace—Platt, the outlaw chief!

Somehow the two had managed to evade Captain McKinney's Texas Rangers. That didn't surprise Brazos. The outlaw Platt was shrewd and cautious; it stood to reason he would have an escape plan. And there was no doubt in Brazos' mind that Lovelace considered himself a gunslinger. How fast was he? And Platt. That Texas Ranger, Hardie had hinted that Platt was no slouch with a Colt. It came to him abruptly that Platt was the more dangerous of the two.

"I reckon yu was right Platt," Lovelace grinned wolfishly. "She shore ain't no boy. Soft and cuddly, I reckon."

From behind the deal counter Casey Sue stood frozen, hardly breathing, heart thundering in her chest. She had to get hold of herself. Brazos needed her help. She slowly unbuttoned her coat and eased the heavy Colt out of its holster. The clerk dropped behind the counter and crawled to the far end.

"So, Kincaid, I heard yu was fast," he said bluntly. "But I reckon I can take yu." In a flash Lovelace clapped his hand to the gun at his hip.

"Look out!" Casey Sue screamed unable to control herself as she thumbed the hammer back on her Colt.

Brazos appeared to blur in Casey Sue's strained eyes. A gun belched red, a deafening boom, and then another even as the first still sounded. Lovelace jerked up with terrible sudden rigidity. Next to him the outlaw Platt staggered backward his dark bearded face changed from frightening rage to an awful ghastliness. His Colt spewed out fire, the bullet tearing a ragged hole in one of the floor boards, and then he pitched forward crashing into a stack of canned goods shattering them across the floor. There was a faint whirring sound followed by a soft clink of metal as a can, spilled from the stack, clunked against the bottom of the door.

Then there was silence.

It was only then did Brazos straighten from his deadly crouch. He stared hard at the two dead outlaws for a long still moment and then he wheeled with pale face and glittering eyes.

"Case," he called and with two long strides he was around the counter. "Are you alright, pard?"

"Y-yes, Brazos," she whispered, slowly holstering her unused Colt. Her face was ashen and her eyes darkly dilated with receding terror.

Brazos gave a quick glance back at the dead men and then with steady fingers ejected the two spent cartridges and reloaded fresh shells before sliding his Colt back into his holster. The clerk got slowly to his feet staring wide-eyed at Brazos and then at the prostrate bodies stretched out in the aisle.

"God Almighty," he gasped.

The front door slammed open.

"Hands up!" a voice shouted.

Brazos raised his hands as slowly he turned his head to peer back over his shoulder. Three men stood just inside the door, all with guns drawn. The one in the center had a pale youthful face belied by a thick dark mustache drooping over his lips. He wore a black city suit and a low-crown wide-brimmed hat. On the lapel of his coat was pinned a six-point silver star.

The other two were less formally attired, both in shirt and dark vest. Each wore a star on their vests. Lawmen, and by the look of them they meant business.

The lawman to Brazos' left stepped farther into the room peering over the rows of merchandize for a better look at the two bodies.

"Hell, boss," he said in a piercing tone, "it's Lovelace and Platt— Daid! Shot clean through the heart"

"Platt?!" the one in the dark suit said in a dry crisp voice as though he couldn't quite comprehend. "Take his gun," he ordered.

Brazos made no move to interfere as his Colt was jerked from his holster. Brazos stared hard at the leader of the trio.

"They drew on me; I didn't have a choice," he said.

"They drew on yu! An yu shot 'em both?! Haw, haw," he laughed. "Yu expect me te believe that. More like yu shot 'em in cold blood. I'm arrestin' yu cowboy. Handcuff him, Chester."

"But it's true!" Casey Sue shrilled.

"Who are yu, kid?" the lawman demanded coolly.

"I—" she began but a sharp look from Brazos cut her words short.

The lawman turned his hard gaze on the gaping clerk. "Yu see what happened?"

The man shook his head vigorously. "I didn't see nothing sheriff. I was taking cover behind the counter. When I looked after it was all over that cowboy was standing there with a smoking gun in his hand and them two fellers were dead where they lay."

"Ah-huh, like I say, yu shot 'em in cold blood. I know them hombres, ain't no man could take both of them in the same setting. Come along quiet like cowboy," said the sheriff. "Chester get the undertaker over here te take care of them bodies."

Brazos made no resistance as they led him away, and Casey Sue could only watch in horror.

"Say, kid, are you gonna pay for this stuff?" the clerk asked apparently recovering from his initial shock.

Casey Sue looked from the doorway though which the lawmen had dragged Brazos back to the items she had placed earlier on the counter.

"Y-yes. How much?" she said anxiously.

The clerk checked the figures on his tablet. "Twenty-three dollars and ninety-three cents," he said.

Casey Sue quickly paid the clerk. "I'd like a receipt," she said. "And would you be so kind to add sugar to that list and deliver everything to the Grand Hotel? My name's Case Thornton."

The clerk nodded writing down her name. He handed her the receipt marked "Paid in Full."

She thanked him and squeezed her way through the crowd blocking the doorway, craning their necks for a glimpse of the corpses still lying where they had fallen. As she hurried toward the hotel she felt the absence of Brazos like the breath had been stuffed out of her.

"Lord, but hadn't he been magnificent?" she soliloquized, eyes blazing in mingled wonderment and revulsion.

Reaching her room she fished out her key and let herself in. She needed to see Brazos, talk to him or she would simply die. Without him at her side she suddenly found herself terrified and uncertain. She sat before the cracked mirror and opened the little makeup kit.

A quarter of an hour later she descended the hotel stairs a little more confident in her boy's disguise, mustache and downy beard in place. She stopped at the hotel desk and asked directions to the jail.

Casey Sue had been prepared for a fight when she got to the jail, but they let her in to see Brazos after confiscating her Colt.

"You can have this back when yu leave," the jailor told her.

Brazos pressed close to the bars so they could talk without being overheard. His eyes were tormented.

"God, Case, I don't know what's going to happen. They got me locked up on murder charges. They're waiting for the circuit judge. And—and I'm plumb worried sick, you all by yourself in this wild town and me locked up in this here jail and powerless to protect you," he said passionately.

"Don't worry about me, Brazos, I can take care of myself," she said with confidence she didn't feel. But Brazos had enough to worry about. "The thing is, we got to get you cleared of these charges. There has to be a lawyer in this town, wouldn't you think. I can pay him—"

"You got that much cash? Lawyers are mighty expensive."

"I brought along a few nuggets—"

"Lord no, Case!" he hissed. "If someone spots them nuggets it'll be all about in a flash that you've struck it rich. You'll be a setting duck. Promise me you won't use any of them gold nuggets."

"I—I promise Brazos, but how am I going to help free you? I don't have enough cash without the nuggets."

"I'll think of something," he sighed poignantly, but it was clear all his once cold poise had abandoned him. "Right now I want you to go back to the hotel and stay in your room—"

"I most certainly will not hide out in my hotel room," she returned, blood leaping. "I'm not helpless. I intend to get you out of this jail."

"Damn it Case," he cursed movingly. "I'll go crazy worrying about you."

Tears glistened in her cornflower blue eyes. "Oh Brazos," she whispered reaching a tiny hand through the bars to clasp one of his tightly.

"Time's up, boy," the jailor announced.

Casey Sue swallowed hard and squeezed Brazos' hand fiercely. She backed away knowing she had to get out of here or she would start bawling.

Brazos pressed his face to the bars watching Casey Sue until he could see her no longer. He turned then and sat down on the narrow bunk. The shock had passed, as often as it had before; the sickness lingered only faintly. Brazos had weathered another stern unexpected happening of this wild country that was the West.

CHAPTER SIXTEEN

Once in her hotel room, Casey Sue tossed her floppy-brimmed hat on a chair and collapsed on her bed. She had found out from the jailor that the circuit judge wasn't due until late next week. For some reason her mind associated the judge with hanging. When her thoughts turned in that direction she couldn't think coherently. She had thought that the Texas Rangers had broken up the rustler gang and had killed or at least arrested Platt. But there Platt had been, bold as brass shopping in MacIntosh's mercantile store along with his sidekick Chess Lovelace. And it seemed to her the sheriff might just have been a speck favorable to Platt, which was sure odd. Maybe he didn't know Platt was a notorious outlaw and rustler.

She suddenly sat upright and swung her booted feet over the side of the bed.

"Think, Casey Sue," she murmured under her breath, reminding herself that she had been on her own long before she met Brazos Kincaid. It was up to her to free Brazos.

That Ranger Captain…what was his name?

"McKinney, that was it," she said aloud as an idea suddenly began to take shape in her mind.

She had to find McKinney, explain the situation. He was her only hope, but finding the Ranger was something else all together. McKinney might have already gone back to Texas. She only had a week before the circuit judge arrived, and then it would be too late.

But if he hadn't gone back to Texas, the place to start looking would be in Guadalupe. That meant a two day ride from here. And cross some wild, frightening country, and this time she would be all alone.

Casey Sue found herself easily falling back into her old cautious ways that first day. It was only natural she supposed, but she missed Brazos something terrible that night as she settled down in a dense thicket choking the mouth of a small ravine where it opened on a shallow stream.

She had been shaken to her depths when near noon she had come upon the burned and jutting spires of charred beams of the old cabin where they nearly died. She had sat her horse for a long moment recalling the terror of that moment, but not able to abide this haunted place, pushed on without a backward glance.

She lit no fire, huddling in her blankets eating one of the sandwiches she had made up beforehand. The cold wind rustled the underbrush and in the distance coyotes yelped. The stars came out, and shivering Casey Sue curled up with her head on her saddle and Satan hobbled only feet away and closed her eyes. Exhausted she quickly fell asleep. It seemed only minutes had passed before she came awake. She rolled over on her side eyes seeking Brazos in the gloom. She uttered an agitated sigh realizing he wasn't there. Should she have told him her plan? She shook her head. No, it was best this way, he was worried enough at it was, and he would probably try to talk her out of it. After a while she fell back to sleep.

She woke in the gray light of dawn, cold and shivering. She pulled on her boots slipped a nose bag of oats over Satan's ears and set about packing her gear, then hunching down in cowboy fashion, ate another sandwich and a can of peaches. By that time Satan had finished his oats. She bridled and saddled the big black gelding and tying her bedroll and pack behind the saddle started off, her Winchester across her thighs. Never had Casey Sue started out on a long ride more keenly alert.

Casey Sue remembered that there was not a single settlement until Guadalupe. She and Brazos had been close to the town, but never entered its precincts. She pushed on into the wildness of twisted, swelling greasewood-spotted ridges and shallow ravines that ran between. When she had traveled this way with Brazos it hadn't seemed this wild and desolate. Oh, Brazos. His name kept popping into her head continuously.

That afternoon she ventured upon what she was sure was the canyon opening leading up to the outlaw camp, but made no effort to discover if she was right, glad she and Brazos had escaped the place. Spotting the opening in the canyon wall alerted her, however, to the fact that she wasn't too far from the town of Guadalupe.

And so, when she rode down a gradual slope to lower ground two hours later and espied the red-roof tiles and yellow stones of the town's buildings from under the overhang branches of scrub oak and cedar, she uttered a huge sigh. She had made it. She stood in the stirrups to stretch cramped and sore muscles.

Casey Sue was surprised by the size of the town. It sported a wide main street, which hummed with busyness—cattlemen, cowboys, women in colorful gowns, and heavily armed, hard-eyed men in rough garb—desperadoes undeniably.

There were several saloons and a bank and she discovered two hotels, both on the main street. After stabling her horse she decided to try the Rio Grande Hotel first as it was closest to the livery stable. She knew she must look a sight, dusty with bits of brush and cedar stuck in her chaps, and smelling of the range, but she dared not delay. If the Rangers were not here she didn't know what to do. She was tired and jaded and worried sick about Brazos. Would he think she had abandoned him?

The hotel lobby was quiet when she entered. Only one person lounged in a rocking chair in one corner, a newspaper in front of his face. She ignored him and marched determinedly up to the desk.

"What can I do for you, cowboy," the clerk asked giving her a quick perfunctory glance. She imagined he was accustomed to seeing ragged cowboys. She leaned her elbows on the desk.

"Say, I wonder if you can tell me," she said keeping her voice low, "if there's any Texas Rangers staying in this hotel?"

"Texas Rangers?" the clerk blurted and his gaze darted guardedly over her shoulder at the man in the rocking chair.

Casey Sue heard the newspaper crackle as the man must have lowered it in order to look at them. The hair on her nape stood up. Slowly she turned to face the man.

"Well, I'll be damn! I know you," he said getting to his feet.

She couldn't help the wide smile that brightened her face. "Bill Hardie," she breathed.

"Case Thornton," he grinned. "I never thought I'd lay eyes on you again. "Where's Brazos?"

Her smile quickly faded. And his face clouded with concern.

"Can we go some place where we can talk?" she asked.

"Shore, come on," he said and started for the stairs. She followed.

"I was hoping to find Captain McKinney," she said as they made their way up the staircase. "I didn't expect to find you."

"Well, I reckon you hit two birds with one stone," Hardie drawled looking back over his shoulder at her. "Captain McKinney is yonder in room 207."

"Oh," she gasped relief taking her breath away.

The Ranger rapped on the door to 207. "Hardie," he called.

The door opened and Casey Sue saw the man she remembered only seeing in the light of a campfire, but she recognized the not so young face, cool and set in an almost stern guise. She saw that he recognized her in the same instant.

"Well, I'll be," he pronounced, an expression of pleasant surprise on his face. His glance shifted peering past her and she knew he was looking for Brazos.

"Case Thornton, I reckon," he said, "Come in."

His eyes shifted over her as she stepped into the room.

"Say, it 'pears you been doing some riding, "You in some kind of trouble?"

"Oh, Captain McKinney, I should smile I am," she exclaimed, unconsciously mimicking Brazos.

"Sit down, son," he said gesturing to one of the chairs in front of a wood desk.

Casey Sue glanced at Ranger Hardie, cheeks coloring. "I don't reckon you know," she said. "I'm not a boy. I'm—a girl."

"Well, I had my suspicions," he grunted looking at Hardie and back to her. "What brings you here and where's Brazos? He's not hurt or—"

"Oh, Captain McKinney, that's why I'm here. I've been riding hard since I left Pinos Altos yesterday morning. Captain, they locked Brazos in jail 'cause he—he shot that outlaw Platt and his lieutenant Chess Lovelace—"

"He did what—?" McKinney and Hardie both exclaimed incredulously.

In a voice over wrought with suppressed emotion, Casey Sue went on to tell of the shooting and how the sheriff had locked Brazos in jail for murder.

"Gol-dang," Muttered McKinney for the moment stupefied.

"Brazos didn't murder them!" Casey Sue said, "They drew on him first; they intended to kill Brazos—oh, oh," she sobbed. "But now they're going to hang him. The circuit judge will arrive in four days. Please, will you help Brazos, Captain McKinney?"

"Calm down, child," the ranger captain said huskily. "Of course we'll help Brazos," He looked at Hardie. "Alert the rest of boys; we'll head out first thing in the morning," he said. "Jimmy and Dale are in good care here. They'll be fine until we get back."

"Right, Cap," Hardie said and hurried from the room.

"Case, you shore are fortunate. Our plan was to head back to Texas a week ago, but two of my rangers were bad wounded when we braced Platt's gang, and I wouldn't leave without them. Otherwise you would have missed us completely."

It seemed the word was out. The handsome lad, Case Thornton, was not a lad after all, but a girl, and a very pretty girl at that. At dinner that night with Captain McKinney in the hotel dining room, the Rangers of Company B stopped by one by one, ostensibly to introduce themselves to Casey Sue, but their lingering and inane comments, finally had Captain McKinney sending them on their way.

Casey Sue went to her room and her bed encouraged by Captain McKinney's words. They would see Brazos got a fair deal, but she didn't sleep well. She fretted over Brazos, imagining him alone it that jail cell. When morning came she was ready to be off.

CHAPTER SEVENTEEN

Midafternoon two days later a group of dark horses and riders started down the wide main street of Pinos Altos. They were ten in number, all dark-faced except one. He was a slight individual, singularly handsome and at a quick glance, no more than a youth with skin very fair and golden curls peeking from beneath the brim of his dark sombrero. The others were dark-clad and superbly mounted on dark bays and blacks. They had no pack animals and each one was heavily armed.

They rode up before the stone jail and dismounted, all but four spread out along the boardwalk silent and watchful. The handsome youth, strangely white of face and dark of eye, joined the other three and they entered the jail.

Casey Sue, standing behind Bill Hardie, peered around him at the occupant of the chair on the opposite side of the dilapidated desk. He had been leaning back in the chair, his boots resting on top of the desk. But at the advent of dark riders he quickly pushed back his chair and swung his feet off the desk, his spurs jingling as his boots thudded to the floor.

"What the hell!" he ejaculated angry gaze darting from one to the other of the intruders before halting upon Hardie.

"Jacobson," he snarled and his hand started for the gun at his hip, but froze as his eyes encountered three drawn guns.

"I reckon that's not my name, Sibert. It happens to be William Hardie, Texas Ranger. And this here feller is Captain Russ McKinney," Hardie drawled indicating the ranger captain with a jerk of his chin.

"So yu bamboozle us all, Jacobson, or Hardie, or whatever yur name," Sibert rasped, eyes locked with Hardie's, hand quivering over the Colt at his side. And Casey heard the desperation in Sibert's voice.

"Don't draw Sibert!" Hardie said piercingly.

The only sound for a long moment was Sibert's heavy breathing, his lean body vibrating markedly. Then slowly he straightened relaxing his gun hand and holding it out away from his body. One of the rangers removed the gun from his holster and quickly patting his waist, pulled another Colt from a cross draw holster on Sibert's left hip.

Sibert's piercing gaze singled out Casey Sue. "Wal, I shore miscalculated yu," he said, and gave a brittle laugh.

Casey Sue jerked the heavy ring of keys from the peg on the door frame and hurried into the corridor leading to the cells.

"Brazos!" she shouted, "Brazos, are you here?"

"Case!" he said leaping from the hard bunk and striding hurriedly to the cell door. "You're here."

"Oh, Brazos, are you all right?" she demanded.

"Shore, I'm fine now, I reckon. Where have you been?"

She uttered a wonderful little low laugh, deep and rich.

"Ah," he gasped, his tight chest expanding in passionate relief, watching as with trembling fingers she unlocked the cell door.

She caught his hand in both hers and made as though to drag him out of the cell. He let her pull him down the corridor to the front office.

"Hold out yer hands," the ranger who had disarmed Sibert ordered, and quickly secured handcuffs on the outlaw's wrists.

"What're yu gonna do with me, McKinney?" Sibert asked.

"Sit down Sibert. I've got a few questions. I want te know how yu got te be sheriff of this little burg," McKinney said.

Sibert dropped into the chair he had vacated moments ago. "I reckon that was Platt's doin'," he shrugged giving the ranger captain a supercilious look. "After we got plum away from yu rangers—"

"Who's 'we'?" McKinney asked.

"Why, Platt, Lovelace, and me," he said, then paused. He took a deep breath. "I should have drilled Hardie. But I didn't remember where I'd run across him in the past until after yu rangers busted in on us."

"Shore, an thet would got a noose around yore neck fer a fact," McKinney responded.

"Ah-huh," was all the outlaw said.

"So, continue with yore story," McKinney said.

"Wal, Platt figured thet me bein' the law here we could start clean pickin' off the gold shipments—say is thet cowboy as fast as I been told?" he asked as Casey Sue and Brazos entered the office hand in hand.

"I reckon there's some truth it thet," McKinney replied.

"Yeah, wal, it all went te hell when thet cowboy gunned down Platt an Lovelace," he said grimly watching Brazos keenly. "Chess shore figured he could take him. I reckon he was shore wrong."

"Reynolds, fer the time bein', lock Mr. Sibert in the cell Brazos just quit," McKinney said.

"Right, Cap," the ranger said and ushered the outlaw out of the room and down the corridor.

"Well, Brazos Kincaid, I reckon I'm shore proud to meet up with yu again," Captain McKinney said reaching to shake Brazos' hand.

"Cap McKinney?" Brazos said, clearly flabbergasted to see the ranger captain.

"Yu shore look surprised te see me," McKinney chuckled. "Shore I wouldn't be here if not fer thet little lady there," he continued admiringly, gazing at Casey Sue. "She rode all the way te Guadalupe; near a hundred miles, te fetch me to save yu."

Brazos turned eyes that shone with pride followed by amazement. "That's where you were," he gulped. "I thought—"

"What did you think?" she flushed when he hesitated.

"I—was afraid—that something bad happened to you," he said hoarsely. "Not hearing from you all those hours."

"I should have told you where I was going, but I didn't want to worry you. And I knew you'd order me not to go," she whispered.

"I reckon you're right about that," he said buckling on his gun belt with its row of brass cartridges and holstered Colt.

She eyed the practiced action of strapping on his gun belt with a tangle of wonder and antipathy.

They rode up the brush and scrub oak spread slope in single file, Casey Sue leading the way with Brazos following with the packhorse loaded with supplies. Brazos stared at Casey Sue slim shapely back swaying with the movement of her big black. Every now and then she would look back over her shoulder and smile at him.

He could not think how to meet the coming issue between him and Casey Sue. Only one certainty stood out clearly in his troubled mind, he would have to leave. And that was tearing him apart. The way she looked at him trusted him—no way did he want to leave; how he would miss her, but he had to. He had his pride, as foolish as that sounded, but it nevertheless mattered. She was rich, the claimant of a high-priced gold strike, and him…he had nothing but his horse and gun, and the clothes on his back. He could not, in all good conscious, sponge off a woman.

Those three days locked in jail had allowed him lots of time to think, and he had concluded after two sleepless nights that he would make his goodbyes, if, that is, he managed to clear himself of the murder charge.

Casey Sue had seen to that, however, once again saving his miserable hide.

Upon seeing Brazos in that jail cell, alive and well, a new spirit had fired Casey Sue, and was now burning within her, unquenchable and unutterable. It had been as though some divine spark had penetrated into that mysterious depth of her, to inflame and to illumine, so that from that hour she was consumed by the intensity of her love for Brazos Kincaid.

But on the ride back to Uncle Josh's cabin Brazos' growing aloofness troubled her. Was he angry at her? Men were such uncertain creatures, she decided. However, she was shaken to her toes two days later when he and Uncle Josh returned from the gold diggings.

"Case, I reckon we got to talk," he said.

"What is it?"

"Sit down," he said and taking the other chair straddled it arms on the back rest. "I been doing a lot of thinking."

For a flash she thought he was going to declare his love and her heart nearly leaped from her chest in joy. But his next words sent her plunging into the depths of despair.

"I figure it's about time I moseyed on—"

"Brazos! What are you saying?" she cried.

"Well, I reckon it's pretty clear. You're set up here with this gold strike, and, and Uncle Will. You're a terribly rich lady now—"

"Brazos, I—I thought we was partners," she implored.

"Yeah, well, you don't need me, Case. I'd just be in your way—"

"Why you faithless, cantankerous—oh, you insult me, Brazos Kincaid!" she stormed blinking at the tears welling in her cornflower blue eyes.

"You're no right to talk to me like that! After all we been through, y-you want to call it quits! Well, I reckon I'm not going to let you. Don't forget you owe me your life—at least three times!"

"Aw, Case, don't talk like that. I got my pride. You know I can't be sponging off—"

"You're an idiot, Brazos Kincaid, and I'm through talking to you!" And whirling she disappeared into her little cubbyhole and jerked the blanket shut cutting him off completely.

razos stalked out of the cabin and walked to the edge of the clearing where he stood watching the gold fade from the tips of the spruces and the sky turn gray bringing a cold breeze from higher up. After a while he walked back to the cabin and sat on the bench as twilight enveloped the little clearing in obscurity. Soon all was black except the space of sky overhead where pale stars blinked, and grew clear and white, and cold. The stillness was something Brazos felt he couldn't endure. A sigh whispered in the treetops as the cold night wind moaned through the forest, and he rose and went inside the cabin and to his bedroll.

Morning found that he was not the first one up. When he rolled out of his bedroll Casey Sue sat at the table, dressed sipping a cup of coffee. Brazos stared at her spellbound wondering at her casualness.

"You're awake," she said. "Good. I've got a proposal for you."

"Yeah?"

"Yeah. You think you should go and I think you should stay. So you're going to draw for it. And not with a cut one way or the other," she said pointing to a deck of cards in front of her. "But you'll have three options."

"Case, what are you up to?"

"Here's the deal. You're going to cut the cards. If the card is between an ace and a five, you leave with only your horse and the clothes on your back. If you draw a card between six and ten, you leave with your share of the gold—"

"Case—"

She held up her hand interrupting him. "I'm not through yet. If you draw a face card, you stay and…marry me. That's the deal."

"I reckon I can't do any of them," he said emphatically.

"Sorry Brazos, that's the deal. It's the cards or nothing. Make up your mind," she said shuffling the cards.

"Oh, no, I reckon not. I don't trust your shuffling. I've seen how you can turn a card anyway you want."

"Then Uncle Josh can shuffle," she said indifferently. "Uncle Josh?"

"I don't know, child. You young folks—"

"Uncle Josh, shuffle the cards," Brazos said.

The old prospector picked up the deck and began shuffling them. After thoroughly mixing up the cards, he placed the deck back on the table.

Brazos stared at the deck, and then reached out a trembling hand. For a long moment he sat thus poised before he shook his head violently. I can't do it," he declared.

"Then I'll draw for you—"

"Oh, no you're don't!" Brazos objected. "Uncle Josh, draw a card. I don't trust you, Case."

The old man's gaze went from Brazos to Casey Sue. "Are yu shore—"

"It's alright, Uncle Josh. Please, draw a card," Casey Sue said.

The old man drew a card from the deck and turned it face up.

It was the Queen of Spades.

"Thank you, Lord—thank you!" Brazos fairly sobbed leaping to his feet and grabbing Casey Sue around her waist and pulling her against him. He buried his face in her golden curls. "I don't want to leave you, Case! But I didn't know what to do! Oh, Case darling. I love you!"

"Oh Brazos, my love," Casey Sue wept, arms snaking about him.

Slowly Brazos pulled back from her, stared down into her lovely face. "Case why would you take such a chance?" he choked. "What if I had drawn a two?"

She shrugged undeterred.

"Hmm," he murmured and drew another card from the deck. It was the Jack of Hearts. "Well I'll be—"

Suddenly he looked at Casey Sue. There was an impish twinkle in her cornflower blue eyes. He drew another card. It was another Queen of Spades. Looking suspiciously at Casey Sue he spread the deck out on the table.

They were all face cards.

"You didn't think I would risk our happiness on the fickle turn of a card, did you? But I had to get you to realize what an idiot you were hanging on to your pride, so I let the cards decide for you," she said and shoving him down on the chair she sat on his lap and proceeded to plant a kiss on his lips.

"Aw, Case darling," Brazos breathed, some moments later as she snuggled close and laid her head with its mass of brilliant golden curls, on his breast.

ABOUT THE AUTHOR

Wayne M. Hoy presently resides in Southern Indiana with his wife of 59 years. A retired Police Lieutenant and father of nine, Wayne has taught a wide range of courses in criminal justice during his law enforcement career. His diverse education has supplied him with an expertise in many areas and he is an educator in the field of Theology as well. In his spare time he indulges his passion for writing and researching settings for his historical romances, which include, The Wolf and the Stag, The Miniature, Appeal to Honor, Banners of Canvas, Fire in the Sky, Lone Star Justice, Ambush at Piñon Canyon, Day of the Outlaw, The Long Way Home, Where Eagles Dare, The Lady and 'The Eagle', The Eagle's Wing, and his latest, Casey Sue Thornton, a Western.

Lightning Source UK Ltd.
Milton Keynes UK
UKHW010652210820
368569UK00002B/35/J

9 781728 369280